C000243512

Terry Steward is an operations manager at a UK regulatory agency. Formerly head of information technology at a national institute, and a former senior biotherapeutics scientist at a major pharmaceutical company. Terry's interests in science, technology and regulation and his experiences ensures Terry is well-placed to generate plots and challenge perceptions in this techno-thriller genre. A graduate of Liverpool University and North East Surrey College of Technology. Terry has a degree in applied biology and a master's degree in information systems management. This, his debut novel, *Novae Spes* was published in 2020. He lives in South London with his wife and three children.

The book is dedicated to my late mother who actively encouraged the writing of the novel and readily commented on the drafts. She sadly passed away before this was printed.

Thank you for sharing your humour and love of life.

Rest in peace, Mum.

Brenda Steward 1934–2020

Terry Steward

NOVAE SPES

A New Hope

AUSTIN MACAULEY PUBLISHERS™

LONDON • CAMBRIDGE • NEW YORK • SHARJAH

Austin Macauley is committed to publishing works of quality and integrity. In this spirit, we are proud to offer this book to our readers; however, the story, the experiences, and the words are the author's alone.

A CIP catalogue record for this title is available from the British Library.

ISBN 9781528935913 (Paperback)
ISBN 9781528935920 (Hardback)
ISBN 9781528968478 (ePub e-book)

www.austinmacauley.com

First Published (2020)
Austin Macauley Publishers Ltd
25 Canada Square
Canary Wharf
London
E14 5LQ

Thanks goes to my family and friends for the engaging discussions and patience in proofreading and assisting in the selection of the cover design.

I'd like to acknowledge the professional work of a creator, Jiovanni Rossi at CrowdSpring, who designed the imaginative eye-catching cover, incorporating plastic items such as plastic bottles within a DNA helix. And although we have never met, thank you Mark Lorche for writing such a stimulating and thought-provoking article in *The Conversation* in 2016 entitled: *Scientists Just Discovered Plastic-Eating Bacteria That Can Break Down PET. Bon appétit!*

Table of Contents

Prologue

It was three months since the four little boats had begun their weekly visits to this remote location. Tonight, was just like the many other nights when the vessels had made their voyage; the skies were clear, with millions of bright stars and a full moon illuminating a calm, flat sea. The air was warm, and the breeze was light enough to allow a wispy sea mist to hang above the slight ocean swell.

The boats formed a rough line astern as they motored quietly through the night, guided by the bright torchlight mounted on the bow of the lead boat.

Each had a crew of four casual workers, recruited from the crowd of men congregating at the harbour, seeking manual work each morning. Most were uneducated farm labourers from the centre of the mainland, displaced and without hope, but in need of money to fill their bellies with food. Any work would do. They sat in silence behind the helmsman. None were concerned with the activities they were to undertake; it was just another job, for which they received a minimal payment.

Bartho, in the lead boat, was the eldest at fifty-five. Having received a relatively good education, he was able to speak both Spanish and English fluently. His seniority and knowledge made him a natural choice to manage the trip.

He knew that the location of their destination changed nightly, and charts and compasses were of no assistance; and, as they had on many previous occasions, they crisscrossed a vague location in the ocean until they found their target.

Tonight, the lead torch picked up their destination easily; seeing the tell-tale mist from a distance in the clear night air. The boats smoothly changed their heading and slipped towards the dark shape becoming evident ahead of them.

'Estamos aquí!' Bartho, the helmsman of the lead boat, shouted as the vessel nudged what appeared to be land: a muted and lumpy, pale, flattened iceberg, occasionally flecked with colour. It stood less than a metre above sea level and was perhaps two hundred metres in width; however, it consisted of neither ice nor soil.

'Sí he llegado Bartho!' shouted a man in the second boat as he came alongside and contacted the land.

Two other boats moored further along the southern edge, about ten metres apart. The crew disembarked onto the "island", which crumpled, crunched and wheezed as the men moved around. Their torches shone across the thick mist hanging over this alien landscape. It swirled around the men's legs as they moved into their positions. Bartho smacked his lips and sniffed, sampling the air; it felt dense and had a sharp acid, taste, far more pronounced since his last visit.

'Bartho, look!' shouted one of the crew. 'Look how red the water is.'

Where the mist had cleared at the edge, a metre below Bartho's feet, he could see in the torchlight how turgid and red the sea had become.

'Si,' he replied. 'Let's get on with it.'

Eight men took up positions around the land mass, at about twenty paces from each other, and extended graduated tent-pole-like carbon fibre rods. The men started to push the rods below the surface. Each shouted out their own assigned number and a value, which was duly recorded by the second boat's helmsman, Roberto.

'Number four: one point four metres.'

'Number one: zero point eight metres.'

'Number seven: zero point four metres.' After announcing his measurement, each man took a stride towards the centre of the island and repeated the measurement process.

Five other men walked around the island with back-mounted metal tanks, spraying clear, odourless liquid through extended spraying arms. Each battered metal reservoir was labelled with a barely legible marking: 'IS-23' and a faded yellow corn logo.

Bartho continued to walk around the perimeter while the measuring and spraying were underway. His felt his breathing more difficult and required more effort; he was getting breathless. The ground also seemed less compact, and more unstable than he remembered from the last visit a week ago.

As on the other occasions, he saw dead fish scattered around the edge, partially submerged in the red foamy sea.

However today he saw more foam, and the pungent, acrid smell was stronger and he saw more fish and birds in all states of decay. Alarmingly, he now also saw large tuna among the smaller fish as he walked around the land mass. He counted three more tuna, many seagulls and several giant turtles. He shook his head in disgust. 'What a mess. No, no, no,' he muttered. He crossed himself and bent to look closer at the turtle's eyes; they were glazed and fixed. Bartho felt saddened and his own eyes watered. He stood back up; his breath was more laboured now; the slight exertion had left him gasping. His own eyes were stinging slightly. *Probably salt from a tear,* he thought, dismissively.

Bartho coughed and became aware of his men around him. They were barely visible through the mist, but he could hear them chocking. Where the fog had thinned, he could make out some men in the distance, Doubled-over, violently coughing and spitting. Bartho looked all round; straining to see through the mist. The movement of the men had started to agitate the land mass, which was undulating with the swell of the sea. Jets of water shot up through the gaps as the land fragments butted against each other. He could see that the men were having trouble maintaining their balance as they carried out their work.

'Bartho, it's breaking up,' one man nearby coughed.

Now concerned, Bartho shouted, 'Roberto, what were the figures?' looking about, not sure where Roberto was.

'Average of zero-point seven metres depth,' Roberto coughed from somewhere behind him.

'Let's get off this "Isla de los diablos", and quickly, it's dropped a metre in depth in the last week alone!' Roberto blew a whistle and shouted, 'Vamos, Vamos rapido!'

The men feeling nauseous and dizzy, hastily started to retreat towards the boats, their heads bowed, and hands over their mouths. The spotlights they carried could barely break through the thickening, acrid mist.

They splashed hurriedly across the breaking land mass, which was becoming increasingly unstable, rising and falling with the ocean swell now further agitated by the men's erratic and desperate movements. Holes formed on the land revealing the darkly stained, blood-red, viscous, foam-streaked sea. Several men fell into the gaps while retreating to the boats. They thrashed in the water, floundering with nothing stable to grab; they uttered gargled screams as the sharp liquid pierced their skin and eyes, and the fumes overwhelmed their lungs. The land bobbed and turned as they tried desperately to get a grip on the greasy surface.

Although some colleagues stopped to assist, plunging their hands into the viscous sea, their attempts to pull out the fallen were futile; their hands were unable to obtain a grip in the greasy water. Soon their skin stung and started to blister. With their feet slipping on the unstable surface, their energy began to wane. With their lungs aching, their efforts unfulfilled, all the men seemed condemned to a watery death.

Bartho staggered into the lead boat and tried to call the others over; he felt the vessel was less buoyant and rocked with his every movement. He saw water at the bottom of the boat; had it been there when they had arrived? It was deep red against the white fibreglass base. He was getting confused. He stumbled towards the outboard and pulled on the cord to start up, and momentarily waited for the motor to start the bilge pumps. He was relieved when both instantly started.

He could no longer see clearly, and he was coughing. Each cough burnt further down his throat. Where his arms, hands and ankles had been exposed to the water, they were painful and blistered.

Through streaming eyes, he saw men fall, and become overwhelmed in the heavy red sea. His vision was impaired and painful; he was not sure of anything; he could not make out details. He felt confused.

Three other men had also managed to return and clamber onto the boat with him. Bartho threw the mooring line off and pushed the boat away from the shore. The little engine laboured in the thick, sea. Bartho grabbed the helm, turning to head away from the mist. He could not see clearly; everything seemed blurred in the dim light. The torch was lost, and he missed it mounted on the bow lighting his path. Without light or a GPS signal to follow, he blindly left the island; he just needed to get away.

The island was breaking up, and Bartho could hear other men screaming and gasping; flailing in the water behind him.

Bartho hoarsely called, 'Roberto, is everyone off? Roberto, my friend, are you okay?'

He strained his ears to hear. The sounds of struggle subsided, and silence engulfed them. Bartho saw the men's spotlights descend one by one to the depths of the ocean, lighting the path behind them. He watched them, falling, falling through the murk behind his boat and down into the depths of the sea like the souls of angels.

There was no answer to Bartho's calls.

The skies were beginning to lighten as dawn approached. Bartho's boat cleared the mist, into open water. He sensed that the sea had regained its previous calm and natural state.

A welcome cool breeze brushed his face, but he could not appreciate the scene. Bartho was slumped over the helm, bleeding from his nose and eyes, and he shallowly gasped for air. The boat had taken on more water. The crew sat, huddled in silence, as the engine sputtered and then stalled. No one attempted to re-start the bilge pump or the outboard motor; they had nothing left to give. Each sat alone, suffering his pain and trying to breathe. All was silent, apart from the rasping of their tortured lungs. They gasped for air with as much control as they could muster; shallow, shallower, until the gasping ceased. And then all was silent.

The sea was calm and quiet under the moonlight and the vault of stars. The air was warm, and a sea mist hung above the slight ocean swell.

Four silent, motionless figures slumped in the boat, as it slowly took on more water.

Chapter 1

Robert put down the document and said, 'Well, that's agreed then. I have an interview on Wednesday on Toby Johnson's Book Review Show.' He waited for a response.

'That's amazing, darling, well done. Freddie managed to swing it in the end?' Turning from the fridge, Lucy put her arms around Robert's shoulders.

'I'm so proud of you,' she said, kissing his neck. They paused for a while, her head on his shoulder, hugging him, enjoying the moment. 'Hmm, it's exciting isn't it?' She said hugging him tightly. Lucy then stood and slapped his shoulder. '...but this won't get the baby bathed, and I've got a flight in two hours.'

'Yes, I suppose you're right,' said Robert reluctantly, following Lucy into the kitchen. 'It's a shame you won't be around for the interview, but yes, Freddie has indeed surpassed herself.'

'You don't need me, darling. This is your limelight, your time. Plus, a wife hanging around might not do much for your book sales,' Lucy said playfully, turning back to the fridge with a plate covered in cling-film.

Robert smiled and opened the fridge door. Lucy was referring to a remark that Freddie, his publicist, had made regarding Robert and book signings. She had said that a single man always does better at book signings. 'Of course, we're not suggesting a divorce,' she had said, 'but play down the marriage bit.' Both Lucy and Robert had scoffed at this and thought how desperate book publicists must be to push sales this way. But these guys were the experts and, since this, his first book, had just been published, he and Lucy agreed they would take any advice on board.

'You can shut it now darling,' Robert regained his senses and smiled at her as he closed the fridge.

Robert looked at Lucy. His wife and friend of some twenty-seven years. She was tall and slender, fun loving and a homemaker. He admired how she had managed to turn her career off as she managed motherhood to their three children, and how she now managed to turn her career back on seamlessly, all in her stride. Of course, he had helped throughout, but he never coped with change as well as Lucy.

Lucy's career as an HR Manager in the Energy sector had picked up since she had returned to her role full-time. She had been requested to stand in for a more senior HR recruitment manager, and she was now involved explicitly in recruitment projects in Africa. These days she had to attend meetings and oversee HR directly. Lucy was now required to travel more frequently between London Heathrow and Nigeria's capital, Lagos.

Robert knew he was going to be a little lonely. Several years ago, their two sons had left to start their own families, and now his youngest; their daughter Jane, had fled to start university. That long enjoyable part of their life had ended. And now they had started a new chapter.

But it all seemed a bit sudden. It had only been three weeks since the house was full; his daughter had been at home, with her friends, and the place was noisy and buzzing with chatter. This had been the case most weekends for probably ten years. They had even noticed that the evenings had become a little quieter since she had left to start university.

He and Lucy had a little more time to spend together, meeting in the evenings, at restaurants, bars and theatres; but they hadn't had long to get accustomed to this change before Lucy accepted the HR role she couldn't refuse.

Robert was impressed with her and proud, but just a little sad; it was all happening too quickly.

He had taken the last month off work to see the publication of the book he had been writing for nearly two years. He needed to be available for his publishers, so he could attend any event they thought necessary to assist the publicity, and ultimately sales of his book.

His manager at work had been wholly supportive too, and he had arranged a temporary promotion for a junior member of staff. The junior's development met strategic management goals for succession planning, so senior management endorsed the plan. Realistically it wasn't easy to recruit process engineers within a food manufacturing plant. Robert had joked with colleagues that this was a 'quiche' rather than a 'niche' role. However, his arrangements had met with universal approval across the division. As long as the contracted production schedules were met, the just-in-time material deliveries occurred, and the preventative maintenance occurred unabated, the board hadn't a problem with the arrangement.

Robert regarded himself as a healthy forty-eight-year-old man. He had no ailments or need for medication of any type and considered himself to be in good shape. Although he was starting to grey around the temples, he was still fit and occasionally enjoyed a game of squash and a round of golf. However, regular physical excursion was not a prominent feature in his life. Indeed, his writing had taken prominence over many weekends and evenings during the last two years while during the day he worked full time.

But Robert would consider a career change, if not early retirement, should the opportunity or favourable financial arrangements arise.

Lucy brought Robert back from his thoughts, 'Now Rob, I've taken some frozen meals out of the freezer and left them in the fridge; they'll be good for the week. So, no reason to forget to eat.' Lucy tousled his hair and whispered to him, 'I'll be back end of the week darling.' She stroked his arm, 'Perhaps we could go out for a meal or meet up with Ted and Louise?' Ted and Louise were good friends of theirs for about 30 years. Ted had been at the same school as Robert and later was their best man. The couple were, like Lucy and Robert, still on their first marriage, a unique arrangement that their other friends had rejected several years ago.

Robert turned to her and hugged her. 'What would I do without you?'

'You'll soon find out,' she quipped, smiling.

#

'5, 4, 3, 2, 1, live.' The sound engineer counted in the new golden boy of daytime TV, Toby Johnson, and the interview began.

Robert was quietly confident; after three weeks the book was already selling incredibly well. Freddie had shown Robert some interview techniques, and Robert had dutifully prepared for the expected questions.

'Welcome to the Book Review Show,' Toby beamed to camera 2. 'Later we'll look at the new Man Booker Prize nominees, but now we have our first guest, Robert Howdon. Who, if you didn't already know, has just published his first book.' Toby paused and looked at Robert. 'Robert, welcome.'

'Thank you. It's good to be here,' replied Robert.

'Now, your book is already receiving some critical acclaim, and it's selling like hot cakes. Tell us all about it.'

Robert was a little surprised at the brief introduction and the rather fundamental question but obliged. 'Thank you, Toby,' he said, 'It's about hope and the new optimism regarding pollution. It's about how we are winning the war in taming our carbon emissions and becoming more aware of our environment; humankind is starting to act responsibly.'

'Yes,' Toby replied, nodding. 'It's certainly a positive and feel-good book, but critics have called it overly optimistic; there have been suggestions it could lead to complacency, and even that it's factually incorrect. Both carbon emissions and global temperatures are still rising. Just looking at this month,' Toby continued, 'we have seen the highest temperatures across the United Kingdom and the longest period without rain in modern history. How do you reconcile this with your good news about pollution and reducing global temperature rises?'

'I accept the criticism, of course,' replied Robert. 'We must not and cannot be complacent. We haven't finished the job by any means; we've only just started to improve. However, I'm more in Steven Pinker's school of thought, in his book *Enlightenment Now,* he explains why our glass should be half full rather than half empty when we consider humankind in the 21st century. It seems that if you announce that things in the world are going badly wrong, you'll have the attention of the news media and politicians. However, if you demonstrate that things are overall quite a bit better than they have ever been, you'll meet a torrent of denial. We are just not geared to accepting good news as readily as bad news.' Toby nodded.

'So, I too am prepared to be the bearer of good news regarding our pollution targets; we have improved, and we are still improving. The rate of global temperature rise increase has all but slowed to a trickle, an amazing feat compared to ten years ago. Although I accept, we need to push this into negative figures, so we can start to reduce global temperatures. The world's annual average temperature has steadily increased over the last hundred years, but the rate of change in the 1990s appears to have been the fastest. Since that decade the rate has slowed significantly. If we maintain our efforts, we will slow the rate even further, until we can reverse the annual increase.' Toby raised his eyebrows and nodded in approval.

Robert paused for breath. 'However, I must disagree about carbon emissions; data from as recently as last week supports the widely-held view that current carbon emissions are at the lowest rate of increase since we started recording in the 1970s. Countries such as Costa Rica are using 100% renewable energy. That would have been unimaginable just ten years ago. Many other countries are heading for 100% power by use of renewable technology.'

Robert was on a roll.

'... Add to that our increased efficiency. We are using less energy than thirty years ago; we have lower heating costs since buildings are better insulated; the use of hybrid and electric cars produce less air pollution. There are initiatives to build hybrid fuelled planes, we are building more renewable energy systems, such as solar and wind farms, there are more solar panels on roofs, there are solar films for office and apartment blocks,' Robert paused for breath...' You can now see all these measures are really having a positive effect. In fact, for a week in 2018, 60% of the UK's energy was generated by renewables, and we've had weeks where, for the first time since the start of the industrial revolution, we haven't burnt any coal in power stations. We have some way to go to catch up with Germany with 78% and Costa Rica with their 100% power from renewable energy, but who would have thought this could have been achievable ten years ago?'

Robert was pleased about the messages he was getting across and the pace of the interview. There were several more questions about how he spent his time and his use of social media; he had found the latter quite beneficial while promoting his book. Then Robert was given a hook to provide another message.

'Robert, given your interest and your positive messages, are there areas that aren't so good? I mean, after this, what is there left for you to write about?' Toby chuckled to the camera 1.

'Toby, that's an excellent point,' Robert solemnly replied. 'Plastics, they are the next goal or rather removing them is. Plastics are the blight of humankind.' Toby raised his eyebrows. 'Toby do you know that the world manufactures over 300 million tons of plastics each year, for use in everything from packaging to clothing? Where does discarded plastic go? Landfill? Ocean fill? It doesn't just disappear! It's a poor legacy for our children unless we provide a solution.' Toby shook his head and looked concerned.

Robert continued, 'Plastics are designed to be tough, and are not easily broken down; they will linger in the environment, littering streets, fields and oceans alike, contaminating every corner of our planet by our addictive use of plastic.

'But we are starting to see some change. Thanks to some excellent television programmes such as the BBC's Blue Planet and other documentaries such as Drowning in Plastic, the public's awareness is being heightened of the effect we are having on the planet. In 2018 people have become aware of the problem of plastics on our planet, the contamination of our food supply, of our oceans, and our earth. But how can we eliminate this popular, resilient and successful product that has accumulated, and will continue to accumulate, in the environment?

'Even slow-to-act governments such as the EU and the UK government are now setting targets to abolish non-biodegradable plastic use for packaging within twenty years.

'Of course, recycling is an option, and with the advent of returnable plastic schemes, this should improve the situation. However, the reuse of plastic is currently at a relatively small scale. I read a report that seven per cent of nationally available PET plastic was recycled. Thus, it is worthy of note that 93% of PET plastic was not recycled!

'But will recycling be enough? What happens to all the plastics we have already accumulated?' Toby looked over at the floor manager who mouthed 'Time' and made a T gesture with his hands. Robert noticed and pulled Toby back from the distraction.

'Toby, as you are aware, there are campaigns to rid the oceans of the plastic debris evident on many beaches, in deeper waters and on our coral reefs. Campaigns such as The Ocean Clean up initiative aim to collect five trillion pieces of plastic from the seas.

'But the world is quite rightly concerned. There must be a way to eliminate this problem. And it must be resolved at a global scale, if only for the sake of our children. I'd even go further and challenge any big petrochemical companies that refine the oil to provide plastics in all their many forms, to actively seek solutions to tackle our plastic pollution.' Toby sensed the opportunity to round the interview off.

'Robert, thank you for joining us this evening,' Toby smiled at the camera and held up Robert's book. This was the money shot that the publishers had wanted, and the sole reason Robert was here.

'The new book by Robert Howdon is titled *The New Horizons: Humans Against Carbon*. It's a really good read, full of hope and a great storyline, although I can't help but think we may see you next year with New Horizons Two; Humans Against Plastic,' Toby smirked.

'After the break, we'll review some nominees for the Man Booker prize, but first these messages.'

Music played, and both men shook hands and thanked each other as the camera panned away; the picture faded, and the advertisements began.

The floor manager walked over to Robert, thanked him and took the clip-on microphone off his jacket lapel. Robert glanced at Toby, smiling to say goodbye, but Toby was busy getting some makeup adjustments and was reading the next items on the script over the makeup girl's arm. The assistant who had brought Robert to the studio reappeared at his side, and Robert dutifully followed him to the dressing room to remove the light addition of makeup. No sooner had the make-up girl finished that the assistant returned to take Robert to the green room.

'Mr Howdon, here we are,' he cheerfully said, opening a door onto a fairly drab reception area or "Green Room" with red vinyl bench seats and some small coffee tables. The walls were adorned with photos of other writers who had graced the Book Review Show, way back from before Toby was involved. He recognised Wilbur Smith, JK Rowling, Dan Brown and, surprisingly, Kit Pedler. He felt a warm glow come over him, thinking that he had become associated with these superior storytellers through a simple interview.

'Please help yourself to a drink,' the assistant smiled, 'and some food. There are hot dishes in the heated trays at the back.' He headed for the door.

Robert thanked him and put his coat over his arm, picked up his briefcase and grabbed an apple and bottle of water as he passed the table on the way out. He paused, looked at the plastic bottle and put it back down. 'I don't need this,' he muttered as he left.

The complimentary ride home, albeit in a Limousine, was uneventful. Robert was still glowing from the interview and the friendly response from everyone he had met at the studios. It had been a great experience, and he was surprised that he had taken it all in his stride.

Celebrity status was currently quite agreeable.

Robert relaxed in the comfortably deeply upholstered limousine seats and pulled his mobile phone from his jacket pocket. He turned off the aeroplane mode and admired the three-year-old iPhone. He smiled. It seemed to be his Swiss army knife for life. He found the internet accessibility, the torch, plus communication and social networking invaluable tools. He read some texts that had just popped up from both Ted and Lucy, the former wishing him luck, and the latter asking him how it had gone.

He had also received some tweets. His publisher had suggested a Twitter account as this could help with the buzz around the promotion of his book. He had some regular followers who asked questions about some aspects of his book or asked for evidence of some of his conclusions, and generally, it was an enjoyable experience, discussing matters of common interest with strangers. One intrigued him; it came from

#LBsavetheplanet, which thanked him for raising the profile of anti-pollution "greenies" in such a nice way, and for getting behind the #eradicateplastic campaign. He hadn't actually endorsed the campaign, merely tweeted that "plastic pollution was the biggest problem for humankind". The tweet finished by stating that he looked cute on the book cover. He smiled at the tweet.

As he looked at his phone, it rang, surprising him, almost causing him to drop it.

He recognised the number. 'Hello, Freddie,' he smiled.

'Robert, honey, how did it go?' His publisher screamed down the phone.

'It went well,' he winced. 'I'm on the way home now. They gave me some drinks and food in the green room and laid on this limo,' he explained.

'Well that's great, honey, they do that, you know.' She raised her eyebrows and shook her head; she wasn't sharing in Robert's joy; if he had been in this business as long as her, he wouldn't be thrilled by a green room, much less a limousine.

'Anyway listen,' she continued. 'You're a lucky boy. You know I've had a request for a book signing in Waterstones in the West End, for tomorrow. You okay with that, honey?'

Robert was about to respond when she added, 'I've already pencilled you in, but if you don't want to, I could cancel for you, but this is the West end!' Robert sensed from her hoarse, smoker's voice that she was reluctant to cancel. It wasn't an issue for him – he had this week booked off from work – so he agreed.

'Of course, I'll do it, Freddie, can you confirm and send me details please?'

'Robert, you're such a sweetie, the schedules on its way. I'll send a car; be ready by 7.30 am tomorrow. It's for a 9 am opening, but you know what the rush hour traffic's like. Love you, ciao.'

Freddie hung up, and Robert winced for the second time; what had he let himself in for?

Chapter 2

The boardroom at GM Agro-Tech was an impressive modern space: stylish and functional, with thick leather carver chairs and a large, shiny, dark wood table. The state-of-the-art flat plasma presentation screen almost covered the whole wall and perfectly matched the Bose teleconference units and Bose satellite speakers.

At the far end of the room, Arthur Tate stared out of the full-height picture windows, down, across the courtyard below him and into the distance. Arthur was a short, well-dressed man of sixty-two. He wore a three-piece pinstripe suit, and silver rounded glasses sat neatly on his round face. His white hair was receding leaving an expanse of tanned forehead.

His eyebrows furrowed as he stared out at the Ivanhoe Beacon on the Chiltern Hills visible on the horizon. Light and cloud played on the hillside and subtly changed the prominence and contours of the slope, temporarily mesmerising him.

In the courtyard below, someone in a white lab coat entered from Arthur's right, and passed through the beautifully manicured bushes, past the Italian terracing, through the trees to the other side of the courtyard. Arthur was deep in thought and barely noticed the person or the courtyard.

Arthur and his colleague, Peter Hadley, had led GM Agro-Tech since its inception, thirty years ago. Both had been molecular biology graduates at Cambridge University, and following their first-class honours awards, chose to combine their funds, reserved for their master's and PhD studies, and invested in an adventure.

The vision they shared was the genetic modification of plant cells to enhance the efficiency of crops. The Plan was to introduce other plant and animal genes to popular crops to improve resistance against disease, which, in turn, would reduce the need for pesticides, and improve efficiency. They had indeed achieved some of their lofty goals: they had improved crop drought resistance; allowing crops in drier climates to be more tolerant of water shortages and increasing the harvest for some of the poorest regions of the world. However, at home, their frost resistance gene in strawberries initially caused a media frenzy, due to the highly publicised luminescent glow the trial strawberries emitted at night. After the furore had subsided, and the aberrant gene removed, the berries were particularly successful.

Arthur smiled; they had learnt a big lesson on quality control, and testing before market! An octopus gene had been identified and used to protect the crops from frost; however, the gene was linked closely to a chemical illuminance gene that was also accidentally introduced into the strawberry plant. Although entirely harmless, the fluorescent fruit caused a media storm. It had been a revelation to Arthur and Peter alike that the public did not want to eat food with "genes in". No one had appeared to inform the public that all food contains genes, or indeed that humans share fifteen per cent of our genes with Mustard Grass or seven per cent with Bacteria. Arthur had learnt that the use of transgenic genes transferred between different species, had been a far less acceptable proposition than cisgenic gene transfer that occurs just within the same plant species.

But learn they did, and subsequent ventures were far more successful. The fourteen million farmers and forty or so million hectares of farmland now growing genetically modified (GM) crops around the world, were a measure of that success, to which GM Agro-Tech has been a small but significant contributor.

However, genetically modified crops still had not been fully accepted by the public or many governments. GM crops were still banned in some countries, and he had learnt that any adverse publicity could seriously influence policymakers, and dent the company's fragile profit margins.

This business isn't cheap, he thought. *A thousand highly skilled employees must be kept busy providing the next beneficial product.*

It was for this reason that Arthur had entered a partnership with another company. Since Peter's death ten years ago, they had been unable to recruit anyone suitable to fill his large shoes. Peter had managed the contracts, all the commercial expertise, in fact. He had provided the enthusiasm for collaboration and determined the direction the business needed. Arthur missed him still.

It was also one of the reasons his nephew, Hugh, had been given a role. Arthur felt that it was an uncle's responsibility to assist his nephew with a break after his difficult childhood. Although he loved his sister, her overindulgence in his whims, and failure to provide Hugh with a male role model, had left their mark. Without evidence of any underlying condition, many people's opinion was that he was spoilt. However, Arthur had developed a specific role for him, to help. Arthur did find Hugh's enthusiasm an asset, however misguided his opinions seemed at times. But Arthur knew that deep down Hugh was smart and principled, although it was hidden deeply behind a spoilt and tempestuous facade.

Nevertheless, as Arthur reflected, he felt most comfortable being 'the Academic'; he was happier tinkering in laboratories than dealing with the distractions of running a corporation and meeting corporate people.

The deal with Butler Oil & Gas was one that Arthur did not take lightly. A good friend of his, Jim Arnold, the Strategic Products Development Manager at Butler Oil & Gas, persuaded him to come along for the ride.

'Arthur,' he had said, 'you have the skills and technology here to align with my company's goals completely. It's a perfect symbiotic partnership; both of our companies will benefit from this. And,' he added rather prosaically, 'honestly humankind will benefit, and we will be appreciated.' That struck a nerve in Arthur; much of the work the company had succeeded in had failed to receive the accolades he thought it deserved, and in many areas, this GM work was shunned or treated as bordering on "Frankenstein" faux-science.

An achievement beneficial to all humankind that would be appreciated was all he had yearned for when he started at university all those years ago. Of course, he wasn't entirely altruistic; he would be grateful for some commercial success! But he, like most scientists, was not driven by monetary gain alone.

There was a knock at the door. After a brief pause, it opened. Theresa, his secretary, stepped in.

'Sir, Hugh is here for the meeting.'

'Thanks, Theresa,' he replied. 'Please show him in.

Hugh strode in. 'Hello, Arthur,' he chirped.

'Hello, Hugh, please come in and take a seat.'

Hugh was a tall, tanned, striking man in his thirties. He had a mop of curly hair hanging over his forehead, and sharp lean features. Well groomed, in an expensive Italian navy suit, with tanned hands that emerged from crisp white cuffs; a single signet ring shone on his index finger. He stood behind a chair halfway around the conference table. He kept his place and looked at Arthur. 'Look, Arthur, I had some thoughts, and before they get here, I'd like us to go through this plan I've…'

'No, Hugh,' Arthur said firmly. 'We've discussed this, let's play this meeting cool, deliver what we agreed to, agree on terms for the operational support and then turn our attention to our next project. Hughes' frustration was evident by his rolling eyes and grimace. *When will this old fool listen to me?* he thought.

The buzzer went; Arthur turned and pressed to respond. Theresa was on the intercom. 'Sir, are you ready to see the Butler Oil & Gas group?'

'Yes, I am, Theresa, please show them in.' He glanced at Hugh soberly, hoping he was conveying 'behave yourself'.

'We don't have any other projects, Arthur; once this takes off, Butler Oil & Gas' profits will soar, and we'll be left behind.'

'Hugh, if I hear this again…' Arthur barked at Hugh as the door opened, and Theresa led in the Butler oil & Gas group in.

Theresa walked in and smiled at Arthur and ignored Hugh. She moved around the desk placing packs of brochures at each of five seats around the table; she then took coasters and water glasses out of a cabinet and set them on the table. She placed a carafe of fresh water at one end of the table.

'Arthur my good friend, how are you?' Jim walked in with an outstretched hand. They shook hands as they beamed at each other.

'So good to see you again, Jim,' replied Arthur. 'It's been – what – a year?'

'Well, close,' said Jim. 'Eighteen months, if you don't count the weekend we met in Tenerife for Charlie's birthday.' He smiled.

'Yes, of course,' Arthur said. 'Yes, that was a good time. Very good.'

'Anyway, let me introduce my contingent; you know they don't let me travel on my own now,' he laughed. 'This is Laura Coleman, our contract Lawyer, just to cover the formalities,' he chuckled, 'and this is Jerry Hawkins, our main Operations Manager.'

Both Laura and Jerry smiled and said hello to Arthur and Hugh.

'And I'm the Strategic Research Manager here at GM Agro-Tech, Hugh Wilkinson. Oh, and this is Arthur, the CEO of GM Agro-Tech, of course.' Hugh quickly added.

All three smiled awkwardly and nodded to Arthur. As they took their seats, Hugh poured himself and Arthur a glass and offered water to the guests. They gratefully took the carafe and helped themselves, passing it on to each other; Laura returned it to the end of the table.

'Yes, hello Hugh. Haven't seen you since your Uncle's wedding, you must have been about five. Is that right, Arthur?' Jim said turning to Arthur.

'Yes, that's correct, about twenty-seven years ago, when I married Elizabeth. Hugh was six and was our page boy.' Glancing around at the others he added, 'As you may know, Hugh is my nephew.'

Laura and Jerry smiled at Arthur.

'I hope you don't still crawl under tables and look up bridesmaids' dresses,' Jim laughed. Hugh looked shocked and unable to respond.

Arthur responded first, 'Of course, that was long before Hugh went to Cambridge and started here,'

Hugh nodded and added, 'And before I did my doctorate.' Calmly and attempting to hide the intense dislike, he had of Jim.

#

Forty-five minutes into the meeting, everyone was holding the corporate brochures, and Jim had started to summarise. 'So,

I think we can now all see where Butler Oil & Gas are going with this. We are uniquely positioned to have a Digester in every country in the world, and we are aiming for at least one in every major city by 2040. Judging by the amount of plastic in the world this will keep us going for at least a century.' He laughed. 'From what I've seen of your work, you have increased the ability of the bacteria to digest three hundred-fold; now the digester can be reasonably expected to provide a return investment within five years, at optimal operations.' He paused and took a breath.

'We are now ready to go live, to start returning on our investment. And you, my friends, will do particularly well. As the sole supplier to us, this contract will provide you with a steady income supplying the raw bacterial material for each digester, and technical support, while working closely with the operations team, led by Jerry, to maintain optimal growth rate and efficiency.'

'This looks very good,' said Arthur. 'You are suggesting a ten per cent increase year on year for the next twenty years, and our production will need to increase to keep pace. This is very encouraging. It's both mutually beneficial, and with a commitment to collaborate throughout the agreed period we should see a return on investment within two years. Yes, it's excellent.'

'Well, gentlemen,' Laura announced. 'If you are agreed, we can sign this memorandum of understanding, and I'll get the legal papers drawn up.'

'Hang on,' Hugh butted in. Everyone looked around at him. Hugh saw an opportunity to impress his uncle and put Jim in his place.

'Jim, you say that you envisage thirty years plus of income for digesting the world's plastic; that's over a billion tons of plastic around the world. And the best you can offer us is ten per cent year on year, from an already pretty low baseline.'

'Hugh!' Arthur jumped in.

'No, it's okay, Arthur,' Jim calmly replied. 'You know, Hugh, you still have a lot to learn. We at Butler Oil & Gas have invested millions in the development and sourcing of the digesters and locations for the initial push, we've had to train operators and engineers, and we had to source researchers to develop the most efficient strains, which you here at GM Agro-

Tech...' he smiled and looked at Arthur, '...have done brilliantly from all the reports I see here. But honestly, you are subcontractors for a piece of specialised support; you are providing a service. You are not critical or our core business, we could source this from others if necessary.'

Hugh stood up. 'Not your core business? Uncle, did you hear this?' Arthur looked stunned. Hugh continued. 'You wouldn't get this from anywhere else. We are years ahead of our competitors. We own, that's us, us at GM Agro-Tech, we own the intellectual property on this modified bacterium, not you. If we drop out of this deal, you'll have to start another research contract that could put you back years. You certainly won't be ready to launch next month.' Hugh leant across the desk and pointed at Jim. 'You should give us a share of the total profit, treat this as a core asset, so you can ensure we are on board with you for the whole journey. You'll come unstuck if we jump ship.'

Hugh looked at their horrified expressions and suddenly became aware of his stance; his outstretched arm and shaking pointed finger. He straightened up and swallowed hard. Beads of sweat formed on his forehead. After forty-five minutes of collaborative discussion and agreeable planning, the Butler Oil & Gas group appeared stunned by Hugh's outburst. Jim looked flushed. After an uncomfortable pause, Jim slowly started to talk, in a very controlled manner. 'That's not how it works, son, and I won't be held to account by a...' Jim stopped and turned to Arthur.

'Arthur,' Jim placed his brochures down and took a sip of water. 'Why don't you and your "Strategic Research Manager" agree on the next steps? We'll wait outside for you.'

Jim was visibly shaken and trying to subdue his rage. He stood up, followed by Laura and Jerry.

All three left the room, leaving Arthur and Hugh alone.

'What are you doing, Hugh? You are going to ruin this with your bloody interference,' Arthur growled.

'You are joking, Uncle. This place would be nothing without my work. I'm working on stuff to make sure we make a mark in the world; we honestly don't need them. I've started scaling up one of our...'

Arthur wasn't listening. 'That's enough! Are you mad? Without this memorandum of understanding, we won't receive the first payments, or indeed the guarantees for continued partnership, which we need. We need it now! And what are you talking about? What stuff?'

Hugh was about to respond when the buzzer interrupted them.

Arthur reached across the table and pressed the intercom 'Yes, what is it?' he barked.

'Hello, sir. It's Theresa, just to let you know the Butler Oil & Gas group have just left.'

Chapter 3

The interview was being aired at 8 pm. Robert turned on the TV, uncorked a bottle of Chilean red wine and placed it on the dining table.

He looked at the ready meals Lucy had left in the fridge and took out a plate, covered in cling film that looked like it contained a lasagne. It was difficult to see through the condensate that had formed while it had been in the fridge.

Robert placed his meal in the microwave for five minutes and went to the remote control to change the channel. *EastEnders* was on, and although it wasn't his choice of viewing, he watched intently for the remaining four minutes of the microwave bake.

Following the ping, Robert took the meal out of the microwave, placed the plate and cutlery next to his bottle of wine and reached for a glass on the counter. A short local news bulletin was on, which briefly covered the Environmental Impact Conference at the Queen Elizabeth II Conference Centre at Westminster, among several other news items. His interview fitted in quite neatly after this.

As Robert sat to eat his meal and watch his televised interview, two other people, as yet unknown to Robert, were also watching with interest.

#

In a subtly decorated room, with fine and elegant furnishings, a woman sat with her feet curled up on a beige L-shaped couch. She gently stroked a large Persian cat laying at her side. Her hand had perfectly manicured and polished nails, and a large sapphire signet ring took pride of place on her middle finger.

The cat purred, and the woman smiled, 'There, there Jessica, he'll be on in a moment,'.

As the interview started, she reached for a glass of red wine and listened with interest. After reading Robert's book and following him on twitter, she was keen to see the man that captured her imagination so.

A single woman of thirty-two years of age, she watched the interview intently. Her pupils and her eyes widened as the camera zoomed in, and she hung on every word he uttered. She felt a flutter in her stomach as she started to formulise a plan to meet this man.

At the end of the interview, she reached for her tablet computer and logged into her Twitter account.

#

On the other side of London, in the near-empty All-Bar-One at Canary Wharf, a smartly dressed, well-groomed young man sat at the bar below a seventy-inch plasma screen. He cupped a cut-glass tumbler containing Jack Daniels, tonic and two cubes of ice. He listened intently throughout the interview with a wry smile. He occasionally tapped the glass with the platinum ring on his index finger. Another man, wearing chinos and navy deck shoes without socks, entered the bar and approached him. They greeted each other and shook hands.

'Hello Hugh, good to see you,' said the man as he approached.

'And you Adam. Glad you could make it, a Peroni is it?'

'Yes please.'

'…and one Peroni please,' Hugh asked the barman. He nodded and turned to the fridge

'Who's this?' Adam enquired nodding towards the TV screen.

'Ahh that's Robert Howdon, the author,' smiled Hugh.

'And…'

'Well he is very interested in reducing pollution and plastics, and he's getting to be very popular.'

'Yes and?' Adam queried again with raised eyebrows.

'Well, I need to plan for our go-live event in a few weeks. I think he'd be interested in our work. It would be great if he could help publicise us in interviews or promote us at book signings. But I need to think of an angle to get his interest. Anyway, Adam here's the money.'

'Great,' said Adam taking the brown package. 'In African dollars?'

'Yes of course.'

'And some for me?' Adam smiled.

'Yes, yours is in there.'

The barman placed the Peroni bottle on the bar. Hugh picked it up. 'Come on Adam let's go over here,' and led Adam over to a booth to talk.

#

The next morning Robert received phone calls from both Lucy and Jane.

First Lucy rang, after watching the BBC iPlayer streaming service in Africa. Robert was in the bathroom, busy brushing his teeth, when she called, aware that the taxi was due in twenty minutes. He put her on speaker.

'Hello, darling,' she exclaimed, her voice echoing in the small bathroom. 'You were amazing. You looked so good in that shirt. Was that the one we bought in Paris? It looked very smart with those trousers.' He put the phone down as he rinsed his mouth.

'No, it was the one I bought in Marks last month,' he replied, reaching for the towel, 'but thanks. The interview went quite well, didn't it?'

'Brilliant. Do you have any money yet from the sales?' she asked. 'Have we enough to retire yet?' She laughed. 'I might join you if we have.'

'Ha, sadly not,' he said. 'I'm pretty much through the twenty thousand advance they gave me, but they said I should receive my first payment after six months. They tell me that I've sold thirty thousand in the last two months. Freddie thinks I should see a boost after last night's interview. How are things with you?'

'Busy. So much to do. But I'll be back at the weekend, so keep Saturday free.'

'I can't promise,' he smiled. 'Life is hectic, and I'm getting offers all the time.'

'Oh, lucky you,' she laughed. 'Okay, I may see you. If not, I'll understand. Bye, darling.'

Robert finished getting ready, slipped on his Charles Tyrwhitt long sleeve check shirt and tucked it into his tan jeans. He fastened his belt while looking for his briefcase as the doorbell rang. He quickly picked it up and reached for his tweed jacket; his mobile phone rang again. It was Jane. 'Hello, Daddy.'

'Hello, darling,' he replied as he closed the front door. 'I'm on the way out of the house; how are you?'

'Oh, I'm fine. Just rang to say I watched you last night. You were brilliant! It was worth all those re-reads I had to listen too. They were so boring!' She laughed. 'Daddy, I'll be home for the weekend, any chance you can pick me up? I've got so much stuff to bring home.'

'Thanks, darling,' Robert replied. 'It will be nice to see you. I guess that's washing you're bringing back?' He laughed.

'Well, yes, but if you come here, I'll show you my digs, and you can meet my friends, and I'll show you around

'That sounds perfect. I'd love to. I'll check with mum, but it sounds good. Perhaps on Saturday morning? Is that good for you?'

'Yes, that would be great, thank you so much,' she replied excitedly.

'Bye, Daddy, love you.'

'And I love you, darling. Take care.'

#

By the time Robert had arrived at Waterstones in Oxford Street, there was already a small queue outside.

He got out of the taxi in front of a line of people. He was unsure which way to go, so he followed the line of people in the direction they were facing. He soon realised that this was indeed the queue for the bookstore and walked along it until he got to the front of the line. He passed a senior woman and man at the head of the queue; they smiled, he returned the smile, and then he tapped on the glass door. Someone in the line behind the first couple failed to recognise him and tutted that he had jumped the queue. Robert thought this was quite ironic, tutting over the person whom presumably they were queuing to see. Luckily, someone inside the store recognised him and ushered him through a side door.

'Mr Howdon?' The assistant asked.

'Yes,' Robert replied. 'I hope you were expecting me?' He raised his eyebrows.

'Yes,' she whispered. 'Of course, but we asked Fredericka to inform you to arrive at the other entrance.' She whispered as though she was in a library.

Robert smiled; Freddie hated being called Fredericka, and she must have given whoever called her that hell.

'We had someone waiting for you, but it's no problem, follow me,' she whispered.

Robert followed the assistant across the store, past tables stacked with books, and pyramids of books stacked on the floor. Robert obediently followed her to the door on the other side of the store. As he approached, he became aware of an arrangement of what appeared to be a minor shrine dedicated to him. It consisted of a life-size cardboard cut-out of him laughing and holding his book, a pyramid stack of about fifty of his books, and a muted TV interview playing on a huge LCD TV screen. To the right of the stack of books was a rather small writing desk with a green leather writing pad and a chair. It even had an ink jar and quill to complete the Dickensian look!

As he approached, two senior staff turned to greet him. The younger of the two spoke first. 'Welcome, Mr Howdon. Thanks for agreeing to sign books with Waterstones today.' They all shook hands. The other man, the elder of the two, continued. 'We've put you on this side so that it's more convenient for you. People can meet you directly from the queue, straight off the street.'

'Then afterwards we can steer them through the store.' The other man added, looking pleased with himself.

Very commercially minded, thought Robert. It reminded him of a visit to a stately home, or museum, or even an airport, where you must pass through the gift shops or duty-free shops to escape.

'Thanks, that's great, good thinking,' smiled Robert. 'Nice touch, the quill, 'I thought they became obsolete with the advent of the fountain pen.' He smiled jokingly.

'Oh, Mr Howdon, we can remove this, we just thought it added a bit of drama and solemnity,' the older man replied.

'Really, it's no problem, it's fine,' Robert replied as he sat. 'Lucky I brought this' he thought, taking his trusted Parker pen from his inside pocket.

The next four hours were probably the most tedious Robert had ever experienced. Inane questions, names to sign that he had no idea how to spell, and the onset of repetitive strain injury from holding a pen for four hours. Something he hadn't needed to do since the invention of the keyboard.

Also, the great idea of placing him at the edge of the store meant that whenever the street door opened, he felt every gust, on what seemed an unusually cold March day. The door had a slow acting closing mechanism too. He was beginning to feel this was a real ordeal; how many book signings would be like this?

However, towards the end of the session, with just a few minutes to go, a petite, well-dressed lady appeared who seemed genuinely interested in his book's message.

'Hello, Robert. I've had your book for a month now, and I wanted to meet the man,' she said. 'And seeing you on TV brought up so many more questions. I had to come.'

Robert drew a breath to reply when the shop assistant tapped him and pointed to the queue and then her watch. She smiled sympathetically. She was obviously concerned that those in line wouldn't get through the signing in the allotted time if Robert started a conversation with this customer.

The lady glanced up at the assistant and then down to Robert. 'Oh, that's no problem; perhaps you could sign it later? I mean, over a coffee, when we can talk?' She glanced back at the assistant as she spoke.

'That would be great, thanks.' Robert stood up. 'Nice to meet you.'

'And you,' she laughed. 'By the way, I'm Lorraine.'

#

Immediately after the book signing, Robert said his thanks to the bookstore staff for their hospitality and for the opportunity to visit them, and then went looking for the coffee shop. He stopped a store assistant for guidance and followed directions to a corner of the store with a small area assigned for refreshments. It was decorated in similar colours to the rest of the store, following the brand, with muted greens and browns, a fondness for dark wood, and ironically it was also decorated with fake bookracks. But it had comfortable leather Chesterfield settees, which Robert liked.

As he approached the counter, the staff enquired if he needed help. Robert declined and looked around; he couldn't see Lorraine. He felt foolish and immediately started to consider why he wanted to meet her. He was married, and older, what was he thinking?

'Robert, hello I'm over here.' At the far end of the restaurant area, in a booth he hadn't noticed, he saw Lorraine standing. She was calling him over. He paused, drinking in the view. She was petite, wearing a tailored camel jacket and dark trousers. She had a bright, elf-ish, mischievous smile, not unlike a young Audrey Hepburn.

He walked towards her, trying not to walk too briskly. *Keep it to a relaxed amble,* he thought.

'Hello,' he said. 'I hope you weren't waiting long?'

'No not at all; to be honest, I popped out to some other stores, and I've only just got back.'

'But please, sit down, let me introduce myself properly.' Robert sat on an adjacent chair and listened intently.

'I'm Lorraine Bellamy, or you may know me as #LBSavetheplanet.'

'The Twitter accounts?' Robert asked, surprised.

'Yes, that's me. I've enjoyed our chats, Robert. We share many interests, and I love that you've brought it all together in a book like this. Hats off to you, Robert.'

She picked up her coffee cup, exhibiting a large sapphire ring on her index finger, and mock toasted him.

Robert smiled. 'Well, thank you,' he replied. 'Who would have thought we'd meet? I've enjoyed our chats online. It's funny you like Dan Brown and Michael Crichton novels, and that you've also just read Stephen Pinker's book. So, yes, we do seem to have similar tastes.' He laughed 'But what brought you here today? You could have just tweeted me.'

'Well, Robert,' Lorraine paused. 'To be honest, there were two reasons. First of all, you are cute.' Robert blushed, caught off guard, and looked down, embarrassed at her candidness. '…and the work I'm currently doing might interest you.'

'Well, thank you,' Robert laughed again. 'But how is your work connected? You've got me intrigued.'

'Well Robert,' she said, 'my company produces bacteria that can digest plastic.' Robert raised his eyebrows in interest.

'I've been working on this for three years now. And now we are scaling up to start real trials in digesting plastic waste.'

'That's incredible! That's exactly what we and the planet need. Did you see my interview? I said exactly that.' He gestured at an imaginary television.

'But what is your company and why isn't this news? Surely the whole world should know about this?'

'Ah, it's not that simple, Robert; until it goes public, the details need to be protected. Other companies could steal our intellectual property and get to market before us. I've probably told you too much. But I wanted you to know that people and companies are aiming as high as you, "wanting to remove the plastic blight".' Robert smiled again. He got her reference to his quote from the TV interview.

'Wow that is incredible news,' Robert was enthralled. 'Are you able to tell me how you have achieved this? Is it allowed?'

Lorraine paused for a moment and replied, 'Hmm. As you probably know, although plastics are an organic polymer structure similar to the natural plant structure cellulose, nothing can naturally digest them. I think you mentioned that plastics are a relatively recent phenomenon; manufacturing only started in the 1940s, and thus microorganisms haven't had much evolutionary time to develop the necessary biochemical tools to break up this new, synthetically organised, organic structure.

'PET plastics or polyethene terephthalate, are the most common types used for bottled drinks and particularly useful for drinking water, they are considered the safest of all the plastics and are the most suitable for food and drink packaging. Also, due to their ubiquitous use, they form the greatest plastic pollutant.' Lorraine looked around and then leant over towards Robert.

'Robert, there's was an amazing discovery: a bacterium named Ideonella sakaiensus was found in the sludge of a recycling centre, and it has been shown to break up discarded PET plastic bottles.'

Robert looked shocked, 'You are joking. Surely not!'

'Don't get too excited yet Robert,' Lorraine smiled.

'A culture of these naturally occurring bacteria take about six weeks to fully degrade a small centimetre square piece of PET Plastic in the laboratory. To improve the bacterium's performance, so we can speed up the digestion process, we have started to modify these bacteria.'

Lorraine paused and looked around and spoke more quietly. 'Robert, we have to engineer this bacterium genetically.' Robert looked confused.

Leaning closer, Lorraine whispered, 'We have taken the genes out of Ideonella sakaiensus and put them into another bacteria called Escherichia Coli that grows much faster. We can get the digestion down into minutes now. Not six weeks!'

'Lorraine, this is incredible.'

Robert was keen to learn more, and excited by this revelation. 'You'll have to keep me informed about all this. You'll keep in touch, won't you?'

'Of course, I will, Robert,' she replied with a coy smile.

'Thank you for sharing this, where are you and your company based?' He started to inquire further, but the older bookstore manager, who Robert had spoken with earlier, interrupted their conversation.

Wheezing and barely able to breathe, he gasped, 'Mr Howdon, thank goodness we found you!'

'What's the problem?' Robert asked, concerned for his health.

'Sir we should have got a photo of you with the staff for the press,' he panted. 'The photographer has just turned up. I've been searching for you over the whole store. Would you mind joining us, please?'

Robert smiled. 'Oh, is that all? Yes of course.' Turning to Lorraine, he asked, 'Would you care to join me?'

Robert held out his hand as he stood, and Lorraine giggled and replied, 'But of course, Mr Howdon, what an adventure.'

Chapter 4

Was it the spring air and blue sky, or the meeting with Robert last week that had lifted her spirit? Lorraine always enjoyed the drive to the GM Agro-Tech facility in her electric blue Lexus. Today she felt even happier as she turned off the main road to the tree-lined "GM Agro-Tech Avenue", a journey she always felt was like a prelude to the start of an exciting film.

The GM Agro-Tech building came into view. The building, built in the 1980s to sympathetically complement the Chiltern countryside, hugged the horizon, and appeared as a long, low, single-storey building, with a large overhanging flat roof, which was supported by equally massive triangular sandstone buttresses at intervals along the building's façade. The facade was predominately blue-tinted glass, only broken by the buttresses, which reminded Lorraine of the sloping chimneys of an American style homestead.

The meeting with Robert at the book signing had gone very well. She felt she had been quite brave going to meet the man she so admired. She had enjoyed his book, and was in awe of his writing; he had put into words exactly what she had often considered around pollution and humankind's efforts to correct years of the abuse of nature. He expressed her opinions perfectly. She liked that he was upbeat and an optimist, plus easy on the eye. *What's not to like,* she thought. But she blushed at how direct she had been over his cuteness. But a woman in her thirties, without any recent success in meeting men of her scientific calibre, and with her current workload, she was proud that she had taken the initiative.

She was also pleased to have accepted Roberts invite to accompany him to the photocall at the bookstore. Robert was photographed first with the bookstore staff, and then he asked her to join him, so she was included in several of the photos.

They did look a handsome couple; her slight frame, shorter than Robert's, complemented his broader, square build. Another picture of them together with the branch manager, in a Victorian style seating arrangement, made them laugh. She remembered having incontrollable giggles with Robert during this photo. She had arranged to have a digital copy emailed to her, which she now treasured.

As she approached the main entrance, the full scale of the building became apparent. It was deceptively large; although the drive suggested a single storey, here, the three levels came into view. These cascaded down the Chiltern Hills towards a valley. Behind the façade, a substantial courtyard, sheltered from stiff breezes, allowed an oasis of Tuscan style trees, topiary and plants in lead planters to flourish. Staff appreciated the fresh greenery and break from the offices and laboratories, and often frequented the area, assembling here on sunny days throughout the year. Behind the courtyard, the roofs of the ten acres of greenhouses were evident as light reflected from the east facing glass panels.

Clutching her bag and coat, Lorraine made her way in through the main entrance. There were other entrances, but she always got a thrill at the impressive reception area. The main lobby was a tall glass chamber, with a round reception desk, a few modern bucket chairs and several large parlour ferns and a full-size palm tree. The wall behind the reception area was a vast, pyramid-shaped sandstone block, with a sculpture resembling a fossil of the company's corn-on-the-cob logo etched in. Impressive as it was, staff working in the area often complained of the hollow acoustics (there was always a slight echo), and how cold the reception area was; the team often wore coats to augment the under-desk heaters battling against the breeze each time the automatic door opened. But even with these flaws the reception area still resembled an expensive hotel more than a research facility.

'Good morning Lorraine, anything to declare?' the security guard, asked as she approached the security scanner.

'No, only my undying love for you, Steve.' They both chuckled. She always felt that Steve, who was nearing retirement, got a little enjoyment from their flirtatious banter. She did.

Lorraine dutifully placed her coat and bag on the trays and walked through the arch. The light showed green, and she turned to pick up her belongings as they arrived from the scanners.

'Take care Lorraine, see you later,' Steve called as she picked up her bag from the tray and folded her coat back over her arm.

'And you, Steve,' she called out as she moved on.

Lorraine walked towards the main building block, passing several long, Italian-tiled corridors that overlooked the courtyard. Her court shoes clicked on the polished floor tiles. Through the windows, in the distance, and beyond the courtyard, she could clearly see the expanse of greenhouses; the area where most of her plant research had been carried out. Although everyone assumed that most of her research around genetic modifications occurred in the laboratory, the results of plant genetic modification were only manifest once the cells and plants had actually grown. Plant growth took time; a lot of her time in the greenhouses.

She passed colleagues, who smiled acknowledging her. She turned off the main corridor, following the sign pointing to the "Bacterial Genetic Modification Laboratories" that were most familiar to her.

Lorraine reached her research area. The first laboratory had a wall of tinted glass onto the corridor, tainting the room beyond in an opaque blue hue.

The laboratory was designed as an isolation room, where samples of plant cells were manipulated to recover specific genes that displayed a particular physical attribute. The process was a mixture of trial and error and involved referencing other scientists work to locate the particular genes encoding for that attribute. When Lorraine had worked on the frost resistance project, she isolated the gene encoding for frost resistance from Squid DNA, but at the time there wasn't always much attention paid to the genes either side of the DNA fragment being removed and put into plant DNA. When the plant grew, and the physical changes started to become evident, there was an opportunity to be surprised! Such as the fluorescent gene that lay near the gene of frost resistance, which only became apparent in the fruit, not in the plant itself.

As Lorraine walked further on, she glanced at the laminar flow cabinets against the far wall. Technicians were busy opening vials of bacterial isolates, and transferring them into selection media in an attempt to grow the cells.

The laboratory was now being used to transfer genes between bacteria and not plant cells. Lorraine found this cisgenic transfer was far more fulfilling; it seemed, easier to accomplish; more scientific papers and references were available, and bacteria growth was much faster than plant growth. The rapid turnover of research provided a quicker route to success or failure. Everything seemed far more efficient.

Lorraine continued walking. The next laboratory focused on the amplification of the genetic code. The genes isolated in the first laboratory were cut into pieces by precise chemical reactions and then mixed with further chemicals and amino acids to increase the number of DNA strands or genes, to be used. These genes were introduced to a culture of bacteria by process of Electroporation, or electropermeabilization, where an electrical pulse is applied to a culture of the bacterium which causes them to engulf the extracellular gene or fragments of DNA of interest. To assist in the selection of bacteria carrying the favourable gene, an additional gene coding for antibiotic resistance was always introduced to the DNA fragment in the process

At the back of the main laboratory, in a culture room, a technician pipetted bacterial cells into Petri dishes. The dishes contained growth media tainted with antibiotics. These were kept warm in incubators to encourage bacteria to grow, but only those bacteria that had successfully ingested both genes would be resistant to the antibiotics and thus be permitted grow.

Lorraine reached the end of the corridor and turned into a locker area; tapped in her security number, and the locker door opened. She deposited her coat and handbag into the locker and bent to pick up a newly pressed, gleaming white, laboratory coat. The coat was embellished with her name and a corn logo embroidered above her breast pocket. Lorraine slipped it on and left the staff area, heading to her scale-up laboratory. This scale-up facility was where successful bacteria strains that possessed the desirable traits were grown from single cell colonies on Petri dishes to one, five or ten-litre volume cultures, as each millilitre of culture could contain up to one million bacteria, cultures of ten litres would contain tens of billions of cells.

Lorraine slid her access card through the slot on the doorframe, and turned the handle; a hiss of air gushed into the room as she opened the door. She was now in her own research laboratory.

Although much larger than the other three laboratories combined, this room was not as brightly lit as the other laboratories, it appeared calmer and more subdued. Glass fronted wall-cabinets contained jars and bottles of chemicals, growth media and cleaning materials, as well as beakers, volumetric flasks and sample trays. A glossy white workbench was fitted around the walls of the laboratory with two other freestanding benches standing at equal distance apart in the centre of the room. Thanks to an HVAC airflow system, the air was pure and a comfortable twenty-one degrees centigrade. The room smelt clean and fresh and the laboratory equipment buzzed with a gentle hum.

Lorraine's colleague, Debbie, was already in the room. She glanced up from her tablet computer and smiled wryly at Lorraine, looking a little surprised. 'Well hello Lorraine, how are you?'

'I'm good Debbie, thanks. What's been going on in here?'

'Same old,' Debbie replied.

Lorraine paused looking at two small, rounded glass bowls with steel lids. A metal frame supported these glass bioreactors, keeping each of them raised above the laboratory bench. The liquid inside looked a dull yellow colour. They were labelled IS-A and IS-B.

'Ah those,' replied Debbie. 'They're yet another attempt at scaling up the original Ideonella sakaiensis culture, but these still don't appear to want to scale up.'

Lorraine nodded. It was a paradox she had seen before. Once bacteria grow in Petri dishes, and a colony of interest is selected and placed in a liquid media, not all of the colonies would actually grow. The Ideonella sakaiensis bacteria isolate had been discovered at a refuge site and was found to digest Polyethene Terephthalate or PET plastic using a unique enzyme called PETase. But strangely this bacteria wouldn't readily grow in standard growth media that E. coli usually favour.

'Just as well we transferred the gene then,' smiled Lorraine, knowing that they would have limited success trying to grow the first Ideonella strain that they knew nothing about.

The bacterial Ideonella sakaiensis isolate had been brought back to the laboratory and passed through a whole process in the other three laboratories to isolate the PETase gene, amplifying the DNA coding for the gene and then introduced it into an Escherichia Coli, or E. coli bacteria.

E. coli, being a fast-growing bacteria, can divide as rapidly as every 15 minutes and had a proven record on scaling up to larger volumes. All the other bioreactors in the room were growing E. coli with the gene coding for the PETase with different types of growth media. Debbie continued taking measurements from these fifty or so, five-litre bioreactors. Each contained a cloudy mixture, and a backlight illuminated the contents that varied in colour from yellow to pink, the vessels looked more frivolous than the bacterial mix would warrant. A small propeller whirred inside each of them mixing the coloured suspension, as air bubbled through the liquid.

'Debbie it's amazing how similar these two gram-negative bacteria are.'

'How so?' replied Debbie. 'They don't grow the same?'

Well, they both have an inner cytoplasmic cell membrane and a bacterial outer membrane, which protects them from many antibiotics like penicillin; it provides the bacteria with resistance to detergents because of the thick outer layer. Oh, and they have lysozyme resistant'.

'Eh?' muttered Debbie.

'The antimicrobial enzyme that animals produce. Did you know that the lysozyme enzyme is found on dog's tongues, it's like an antiseptic, but gram-negative bacteria are resistant to this.'

'Thanks, Lorraine, very interesting,' Debbie replied sarcastically, with a smile and a twinkle in her eye.

Lorraine watched as Debbie moved to the next bioreactor, and noted some output figures from bioreactor 23; she smiled and whistled. She then continued to the other vessels in the room.

'What's that whistle for Debbie?

'This very first E. coli that became transfected with the PETase.'

'Really? Why are we wasting time with that? I thought that it had failed to grow?' Lorraine said dismissively.

'Well I kept it running, and now they appear to be growing incredibly fast, it's remarkable,' Debbie continued. 'After being dormant for weeks, it's now breaking down plastics here at an unprecedented rate.' Lorraine walked over to take a closer look. 'When we received this unmodified Ideonella sakaiensis IS strain a year ago, the low enzyme levels meant that it would take six weeks to dissolve the standard plastic PET sample. Since we've spliced the gene and introduced to Escherichia Coli, the enzyme rate is enhanced. Look at the data here, the digestion is now occurring in 45 minutes, and the bacteria are doubling in number every 25 minutes. The rate is startling.'

'That is remarkable, but we have better, newer strains coming through in the digesters,' Lorraine added. 'They don't produce by-products.'

'True,' answered Debbie. 'This one stinks and pits the metal propeller blades. It is also producing a lot of acid.'

'It is impressive,' agreed Lorraine, 'but that is the old strain, we are not using it now so we could use the space for growing up more of the newer test cultures?'

'Ok I will do,' Debbie replied nodding. She then smiled and added, 'But Lorraine why exactly are you in today?'

'Why not? Weren't you expecting me?'

'No, it's just that I saw the photos of you and Robert Howdon and I thought maybe you'd been whisked off your feet,' she laughed.

'What photos?' Asked Lorraine, becoming slightly flushed. Debbie went to an adjacent room and brought a newspaper into the laboratory.

'Here, look. It's not front-page news, but look.' Debbie showed her the article and the photo of all of them at the Waterstones bookstore on Friday. Robert and Lorraine were in the centre of the picture.

'Wow, that's quick,' said Lorraine. 'That was only taken Friday afternoon.'

'What's he like?' asked Debbie

'He's very nice, charming and of course very well read,' Lorraine reflected. 'I'll hopefully see more of him.'

Debbie giggled, and Lorraine joined her. It hadn't come across quite as she intended.

'Husband material do you think?' enquired Debbie deeper.

'Well let's say that I'd consider it,' laughed Lorraine. But changing the subject quickly she asked:

'Right Debbie, err sorry, but can you give me an update on current production, our bulk-ups and shipping orders, please. We go live at the production site in a fortnight, and I want to be sure all is on schedule.'

'Sure,' replied Debbie, 'Production tests here have been pretty good; well brilliant, actually, Look.' Debbie showed Lorraine the growth charts for each of the bioreactors and flipped back several pages.

'I've seeded all the bio-reactors with the second batch of fifty of the different genetically modified bacterium we identified last month. They're all labelled IS-42- to IS-91. All of these have good growth rates and produce high levels of PETase.

'Some of these had increased tetrahydride acid levels and elevated ethylene glycol.'

'Hmm this acid will limit the growth of the culture; the medium will become too toxic for the culture,' said Lorraine pointing to the corresponding charts of growth rate.

'Look again,' Debbie continued, turning back to recent data. 'That's what I thought, certainly the older strains exhibited those characteristics, so I changed the growth media and repeated the procedure in this batch of test media. By adding alkali to neutralise the increase of tetrahydride acid produced, the digestive rate continues to increase as the population doubles.'

'Now that is impressive,' nodded Lorraine. 'Have all these received the PETase modifications to further breakdown and digest the Xylene and tetrahydride acid, once the plastic supply is exhausted?'

'Yes,' Debbie replied. 'Some are totally digesting plastic to CO2 and water, but some media is getting too toxic before they can switch to xylene and acid breakdown, and the bacteria die. That's where the alkali helps to neutralise the acidity and raise the Ph.'

'Debbie this is good work, regardless of the end products they're all digesting plastic. They've all had the antibiotic resistance gene removed ready for bulking up and shipping. If we can repeat this in the digesters at this rate, we could probably digest a ton of plastic within a week, with no toxic by-products. Can you document the alkali control and we'll pass the information to the operations manager at the production site?' Lorraine smiled. 'Ah, which reminds me; have we started bulking up some test cultures to ten litres yet, ready for dispatch, production wants some material to start testing the digesters?' She looked around for the dispatch sheet.

'Yes, of course, where have you been?' Debbie laughed. 'Oh, I know. The book store!' she laughed again. 'Well, we started producing these last month. About five batches have gone.'

'Gone? Gone where?' Lorraine asked.

'Here,' Debbie picked up the dispatch sheets. She showed Lorraine the order request form, and the attached dispatch record and the sign-off dates. They had started on the 10th of February.

'But I didn't know they were ready for them yet. Production trials are not due until April, and we should use the latest strains to bulk up.' Lorraine looked down the list and saw fifteen dispatches, all for Port Bata, and the last five for San Carlos in Equatorial Guinea. 'Who authorised these?'

'Hugh arranged it, see?' Debbie said pointing to the despatch request.

'He said they were needed urgently for testing.'

'Hmm. Thanks for this. I need to find out what's happening,' replied Lorraine. 'Can you tell me what type was sent?'

'Well, all ten batches apart from the last five were this one,' she pointed to IS-23. 'But the last five batches sent were this one.' Debbie pointed to the chart. 'IS-48. It's by far the best.'

'The IS-48 is no problem; this is the best yet, and it can go out to production if they are ready. Have they both had the antimicrobial selection pressure removed?' Debbie nodded and then shrugged. 'Actually no, I don't think the IS-23 has.'

'And the IS-23, remind me again, was that the corrosive one?'

Debbie responded, 'Yes this is one of the earlier strains, around the 20s, they overproduced tetrahydride, and this strain didn't have the modified PETase to break further down to CO_2 and water, plus these are quite toxic, and turned the bioreactors acid indicators bright yellow,' Debbie replied. 'It smelt disgusting; do you remember?'

'Yes. But why on earth did these ever get dispatched?' asked Lorraine. 'These were test ones for reference not to be used anywhere, and they still have the antibiotic resistance?' Lorraine queried. Debbie shrugged and shook her head. 'Hugh just wanted something to test, I have no idea what stage it was at.'

'But he's sent an aggressive bacterial strain out of the country, and it still has antibiotic resistance.'

Lorraine was getting concerned and paused to gather her thoughts. She turned to Debbie, 'Could you contact the Operations Manager in Equatorial Guinea to confirm what strain he received, please?'

Debbie sensed some urgency and nodded. 'Yes of course.'

#

Lorraine was suspicious when she received a call from Hugh to meet at the central campus offices later that day. Although they had studied together for a period, and even hooked up socially in the early days, she found his hot-headedness and arrogance too tiresome to put up with. Lorraine had to let that relationship go, and now they actively avoided each other. She could understand how he'd got to be Strategic Research Manager, though; he was smart, shrewd, and always found a way to succeed; he wasn't modest at taking praise and credit for others' work or indeed stepping back from accountability when things went awry. His nickname of Mr Teflon was apt and made Lorraine smile. Apart from some corporate meetings, it had been a year since their last brief encounter.

Today she had been summoned to his office, and now she wanted to speak with him about the batches to Equatorial Guinea.

Lorraine walked along the corridor towards reception and climbed the stairs to the administration and corporate areas on the second floor

'Lorraine.' Hugh stood and smiled as she entered his office. The room was typically Hugh. It was larger and more expensively decorated than any other she had seen on campus and had a beautiful vista of the Chiltern Hills, just a mile away.

Hugh was immaculately dressed, perfect looks and smile and exuded confidence from every pore.

Hugh made an uncomfortable attempt to hold both of her arms to hug her. But Lorraine resisted and stepped back, putting her hand out to shake. She didn't feel any need to embrace. They shook hands.

'Hugh,' Lorraine said, standing upright, rather primly. 'What do you want?'

'Well, Lorraine, please indulge me here,' he smiled. Lorraine nodded and looked at her watch.

'Err you're looking very nice!' he exclaimed.

'Please get on with it Hugh.'

'Yes, of course. We've both been here for, what? Seven years?'

'Eight,' she replied.

'Ah, yes, you started before me, and you were working in the gene modification suite within crop research centre?'

'Yes,' she replied. 'It was for the frost resistance gene in wheat.'

'Exactly,' Hugh added quickly. 'And all that research, successful as it was, was treated with disdain by food producers and by the scientific community, and the green brigade to boot. All that research and investment, all that work and the potential benefits to humanity, and yet none of it realised.'

Lorraine's heart sank. Where was he going with this old news? 'Yes Hugh, but there was a reason for that: unstable and harmful by-products, such as enzymes that we weren't aware the genes would code for, that could have been dangerous. We needed to show due diligence, and we weren't sure how safe they were until tests had been completed, and then there were some ungoverned trials, which caused some concerns regarding the effects on pollinating insects. That's why we had to cordon some areas off for small scale testing…'

'Lorraine, of course, there will be some minor casualties en route. You can't make an omelette without breaking an egg,' Hugh quipped dismissively. 'But honestly Lorraine, sometimes I wonder whose side you are on. What's the point of jump-starting evolution with genetic modification if we end up testing in real time, in cordoned off areas, or trials? It would take as long as evolution itself to get anything approved. Governance has no role in research and development; in fact, governance kills innovation.'

Lorraine sat down and sighed. *This could be a long meeting,* she thought, observing him quietly; his voice was starting to rise. She'd been here before, and although she wasn't frightened, his temper seemed to be more volatile than she remembered. Was he under pressure, or stressed, she wondered?

After a breath, he started again. 'Okay, you know a lot of those media news stories on GM crops were unfounded and scare tactics, don't you?' He glanced at Lorraine. 'Some probably started by our competitors. However,' Hugh drew a long breath. 'However, we are now in a new space. The work, you and your team, are doing is revolutionary, it's bloody brilliant! The same work you did on crops but now applied to bacteria, will be seen as humankind's saviour in the fight against plastic pollution. It's a new hope; it's our Novae Spes.'

'Yes,' Lorraine agreed, smiling, not quite understanding his theatrical use of Latin. 'We are making good progress. This week we singled out a test strain that is more resilient to ph and pressure, and continues to digest…'

'Lorraine,' he interjected.

'I have a proposal for you.' Lorraine looked up with a frown, wondering what was coming next, as Hugh walked to his desk.

'What if I arranged a doubling of your current budget and staff? I bet that would help you meet your targets.'

'Well yes,' she replied. It had been no secret that in the last three years she had worked on this project she had neither the equipment required or a full contingent of staff; everything she had been scavenged or taken from other unrelated projects.

'Yes, that would be great, that would allow us to perfect the…'

'Lorraine you know that production goes live in several weeks at our production facility at Equatorial Guinea?'

'Yes,' replied Lorraine. 'Actually, I wanted to bring up that the…'

'Thank you, Lorraine,' Hugh interrupted. 'Let me finish, please. The production facility opens in a fortnight for full-trials, we need some publicity, to impress the consortium and Arthur, he…' He paused, 'Anyway, I was thinking of asking Mr Robert Howdon the author. The man of the moment with TV interviews

53

and book signings, who also has an interest in environmental issues and reducing plastic pollution.' Lorraine's eyes widened when he mentioned Robert. '…and I would like to ask him if he would be interested in helping us with some publicity and endorsements.'

Hugh pushed a newspaper across his desk, showing the same picture Debbie had shared earlier. 'Lorraine, I see that you have met him. You know you make a great couple,' he smiled. Lorraine looked uncomfortable and fidgeted on her chair. He continued.

'I'd like to increase your budgets and resource, but there is something I need you to do for me.'

Chapter 5

It had been five weeks since Jane had seen Mum and Dad. They had driven her to Plymouth at the start of term. Jane had shown them around the campus, the common rooms, the canteen, lecture facilities, laboratories and deep-water tanks.

Dad seemed impressed with the marine and diving facilities, and Jane had arranged for him to meet her year tutor. 'The Prof' – Professor Wilmsford. Jane had mentioned to him that her father had recently been interviewed on TV to talk about his new book and The Prof was keen to ask questions.

They had common interests; Dad worked in a food manufacturing process and production area and had trained as a scientist. Recently dad had developed a keen interest in controlling pollution. As The Prof was studying and lecturing on the effects of marine pollution, they seemed to have some mutual areas of interest. The Prof had shown Dad the deep-water tanks and the facilities, and dad had commented on how impressive the facilities were, with the latest analytical equipment. 'Good to see the fees being put to good use,' Jane had heard him say.

Jane had then shown Mum and Dad her accommodation and introduced them to her flatmates, and some of their parents who were also visiting. Mum had said later, on the way to the car, that she was shocked that such dirty and shabby facilities could cost so much. 'The landlord has a lot to answer for!' she had said, much to Jane's embarrassment. To make matters worse, Mum had also purchased some cleaning materials at the local shops and started to clean up the bathroom and kitchen.

But for the money and the budget she had, it was all worth it. Jane had been interested in biology and then marine biology. To study at her chosen university and to rent her own digs was all she wanted.

When Jane reflected on how she became interested in marine biology, she thought back to her childhood when Mum and Dad took her and her brothers on holiday, playing in the sea, going on snorkelling excursions, paddling and exploring rock pools armed with a fishing net.

Plymouth University had been her goal since she began studying for her "A" levels. In year eleven the school had arranged a presentation from one of the university tutors, and she loved the idea of a job that she always associated with her holidays. The facilities and the International Curriculum appealed to Jane's sense of adventure, and she felt she'd get the right balance of activity between lectures and studies. Jane still thought that her BSc (Hons) in Ocean Science and Marine Conservation was a good choice of degree.

The fact that some friends had recommended the university based on the social and party scene 'had nothing to do with my choice', she always insisted with a tongue firmly in her cheek.

She had only recently discovered that she was privileged, as a year one student, to be selected to attend year three's field study, an expedition to Equatorial Guinea, arranged by The Prof. The group would analyse water samples, assess the impact of pollution and monitor the variety and number of local marine species.

She'd googled the location, and found that Equatorial Guinea was somewhere on the west coast of Africa and she had seen that the climate, being near the equator, would be hot and humid, with frequent rain. Jane knew that this included time on the seashore among the ocean breezes, which also meant frizzy hair! She would have to take hair care products! All weather clothing was essential, so Jane had packed plenty of changes of clothes and factor-fifty skin protection.

The University of Equatorial Guinea, known locally as Escuelas Nauticas Bata, was hosting the visit. Reciprocal arrangements were arranged at Plymouth at various time of the year, with this university and with others around the world.

#

On the day, Jane left the campus with eight other Marine Biology year three students, whom she barely knew, and two lecturers, The Prof and Julia Johnson. They flew from Exeter Airport to Paris and changed at Charles De Gaulle Airport to fly to Port Bata, Equatorial Guinea. They arrived at 5 pm in a warm and balmy Port Bata at a small international airport surrounded by palm trees.

Just as they passed through the arrival's hall, they were whisked off in a minibus to the university campus at Escuelas Nauticas Bata, where they were met by the local year tutor, Pierre Castrol, who warmly greeted them, and introduced them to a junior lecturer, Juan. He was a short, athletic and enthusiastic local man in his mid-twenties. He smiled broadly and was friendly with all the students. Jane immediately liked him and hung on to his every word as he showed the students the accommodation and guided them to their rooms.

Their accommodation was in the single-storey student block, made available while the local students had vacated due to their own excursion to Antarctica. *I must go there some time,* Jane thought.

For their part, the university had coerced Juan Dougan to be a chaperone and guide; to show the students around the area, assist with transport arrangements and help with translation from the local pidgin Spanish, which many English visitors found difficult to understand fully.

Once all the introductory tours had been completed, Juan brought everyone to the lounge in the accommodation block. He then formally introduced himself to the group and went through the itinerary.

'Hello, my friends. As you now know, I'm Juan. Pleased to meet you all and I hope you have a very enjoyable time here in Equatorial Guinea, at Port Bata and our university, Escuelas Nauticas Bata.

'This afternoon, you can all settle in and unpack. Please aim to meet downstairs in the canteen area for our evening meal at 7 pm. There will be a presentation on the week's activities, and you'll be able to register and get the appropriate kit assigned.

'Each morning, I plan to take you exploring the coast, taking samples and carrying out some analysis. We'll look at flora and fauna and spend time identifying types of pollution, classification and some statistical analysis.

'If this all goes to schedule, we can have a day off on our third day. You can sail with me, spend time on campus or relax around the town.

'After dinner tonight, please go to one of the check-in desks, listen to what the activity entails and register your choice.

'The sailing is generally good; we may see some larger species such as dolphins, turtles, tuna, and occasionally whales and sharks.'

The group looked excitedly at each other and started chatting; this option seemed the most exciting one.

#

Jane's first day flew past. She had spent her time crawling around rock pools; overturning rocks and collecting shells. She took water, seaweed and sand samples, dug holes in the sand and collected some mollusc samples. She decided she hated seaweed; it was slimy to the touch, and it stank when it started drying up. The day was pretty much-spent sampling, such that by the afternoon she was beginning to feel tired and a little bored of it. Luckily her mobile phone brought some much-needed relief, and she discretely used it to alleviate the boredom by posting on social networks with some photos.

On the second day, Juan introduced them to Malboa Beach, a once idyllic spot that was now strewn with litter. Juan asked that they peg out a three-metre-square area and remove every piece of litter from that area. They were to place all the items they had gathered into metal cages positioned higher up along the beach.

Jane was thinking, 'What are we doing? Clearing up other people's mess?' But after several hours she was quite proud of her clear patch of beach. She posted some pictures and 'feeling proud' statements on social media. The group's efforts looked impressive next to the mess that remained on the beach.

For the next three hours, all the students had to take further samples of their patch of beach. Again, they collected water, sand and mollusc samples.

They all noticed how many fewer molluscs and shells they collected on this cleared land.

'Come over here,' Juan called.

He was standing next to his red pick-up truck. The rear tailgate was folded down and a silver box with a black window, similar to an upturned microwave, was resting on the tailgate.

A power pack sitting on the ground below the tailgate powered the unit.

'Gather round,' Juan called. 'We're using an analyser to give us an indication of the amount of micro-plastics in the environment here. As you know from your class notes, Microplastics are small plastic fragments, smaller than 5 millimetres in size, much smaller than the pieces you have cleared today. They can come from raw-plastic pellets or "nurdles" used to manufacture plastics, microbeads used in shampoo, face-scrubs, and detergents; they are shed from clothing, they are used in drug delivery and used to blast the hulls on boats to clean them, to name just a few examples. But the majority of them come from the degradation of plastic into smaller fragments of plastic.'

'Plastics bob around in the ocean for a long time, but in that time the wind, the sun and rain will erode them, breaking them up into smaller pieces until they become micro-plastics.

'The harm to the environment is two-fold:

'First, the plastic fragments are eaten by animals as food, but are not digested; they fill the animal's stomach, making the animal feel full, and preventing any other food getting in. The animals end up starving to death.

'Secondly, the tiny micro-plastics absorb other harmful chemicals, which will then transfer to animals' fatty tissue, causing cancers, reproduction problems, deformity and eventually death.

'When you buy or eat a fish meal, you might not know the amount of toxins within the fatty tissues, but when we digest the fish, chemicals and pollutants are released and then absorbed into our own fatty tissue. In time it will be possible that humans will suffer the same consequences as sea animals such as the dolphins, seals and tuna that eat smaller fish that have eaten toxic micro-plastics.'

The group was stunned into silence. Juan sensed the atmosphere – as always this was a difficult lesson to grasp.

'But cheer up,' Juan tried to change the mood, 'you are the guys that can do something about this. As with most things, we need to find out something is happening before we can correct it. Am I right?' Students nodded, as he looked around, nodding back at them. 'Yes, and this machine tells us what we have.'

He walked over to the cleared patch and scooped up a beaker of sand. 'Look,' Juan then said. 'Look in this sand. It's not all sand.' The students stared into the beaker and indeed saw small spots of plastic, like breadcrumbs, mixed into the sand.

Juan poured the sand onto a white tray, and the number of micro-plastics became more evident. Although the pile was primarily sand, there were many, many, plastic pellets. 'These smaller micro-plastics are about the size of zooplankton and get in the food chain as larger filter feeders like whales and fish scoop them up with their regular food.

'This machine will count the plastic pellets against the amount of sand and give a ratio.

'Then the analyser will provide a rough analysis of the pollutants that can be found within the sand, and within the plastics.

'This analyser takes the 100-gram sample of sand; it adds water and mixes. The plastic will float off the sand, and then the plastic is skimmed off, away from the sand, and dried in a tiny oven. The analyser then gives a dry weight value for the plastic. Knowing the weight of the sand that was added, we'll have a value for how much plastic is in the sample as dry weight by weight comparison.'

Juan added 100 grams of sand to the analyser and pressed start.

The machine started whirring, and Juan turned to the group. 'Anyone have any questions?'

There was a pause, and a student at the front put his hand up. 'Juan, what about when you are at sea, how would you know what amount of micro-plastics were in the water?' he asked.

'Good question,' Juan replied. 'At sea, you can drag a small mesh net behind boats and then take the plastic out and add it to the machine so that the dry weight can be calculated. You compare that to the volume of water that passed through.'

'Juan?' Another student at the front asked.

Juan nodded at him. 'Yes?'

'We saw some dead birds and a turtle on the beach. Do we know what killed them? I mean could it have been plastics or chemicals?'

'Another good question,' replied Juan, squinting in the sun. 'Let's go and find out.'

Juan, along with the students, headed over to a patch of beach that hadn't been cleared. There was a dead seagull here.

'Stand back, and look away if you are squeamish,' Juan said. Several students turned away.

He laid the seagull flat and waved some flies away. Juan pulled a small flick-knife out from his pocket and, while kneeling, swiftly cut the seagull from the neck down to the tail. More of the students looked way.

Jane continued to watch; she was amazed as an assortment of different coloured fragments spilt out from the stomach. They were unmistakably plastic. Although disgusted, she took a picture and posted it.

'I'd guess that this seagull starved, it couldn't eat as its belly was full, but it wasn't food, it was plastic,' Jane said solemnly.

'Yes,' agreed Juan. 'Sad, poor bird.' Jane posted a photo with :o(.

A beeping noise came from the analysers. 'Ah, let's go see the results,' Juan said, standing up.

A paper ticket hung from the analyser.

'Ok,' Juan said, tearing the paper off the analyser. 'Plastic dry weight was 11 grams from one hundred grams of sand. That suggests that 11% of the sand on this beach is actually plastic. Now we know that this beach is particularly polluted, but 11% is a huge amount. Especially if you think that every beach on the earth could contain 11% plastic; it could be stirred up by the tides and waves and mixed into seawater. Animals and birds would ingest this. This is worrying; if this keeps up, we could kill off all of our sea-life.'

#

The following day, Jane stood with other students on a palm tree-lined beach just south of Port Bata. They were in the shallows of the clear, cool sea that lapped at their feet. The group were standing next to a large white catamaran sailing boat. It stood proud and gleaming in a blue sea, bobbing with the light breaking waves. Aboard it was a worker from the marina, who leased the sailing boats out. He was going through his contractual obligations, checking everything was working: that the diesel engines worked, the tanks for water and fuel were full, and the safety equipment was sufficient for a group of seven. He then ordered that the students respect what was an expensive sailing yacht. He explained the layout, and how to treat the boat properly, and instructed them to 'listen to the skipper', and gave out some other dos and don'ts. It was as though he was reading from a script, and along with his broken English, the students soon lost interest. But Jane understood that this boat was a Spirited Catamaran 420 Crossover. It was forty-four-foot-long and had eight berths or beds, and a 'head in each hull'. Jane thought she must ask what that meant.

When he had finished his sermon, he jumped down and shook Juan's hand and patted his shoulder, and they both laughed, 'But my friend,' he added, 'please stay clear of the rubbish patch, you will damage the boat.'

'Of course,' replied Juan. 'I've never seen it around here it must be further out to sea.'

'We have had a storm out at sea that has brought strong onshore breezes. It could be closer than you think.'

'Ok thanks,' Replied Juan.

'Hasta luego amigo,' he replied. 'Stay clear of any mist my friend,' he added.

Juan then instructed the students to board the catamaran at the steps at the back. One by one they boarded and stood in a room in the middle of the vessel. This saloon consisted of a large semi-circular settee next to a large round table. The table stood by a window stretching the width of the boat, pointing towards the front or "bow" of the boat. Beyond, Jane could see the two hulls, and a net across them, traversing a beautiful aquamarine sea below.

Juan continued the safety tour. 'The safety jackets are here and here.' He pointed to two chests on the floor. 'You may choose to wear them at any time, but if things get dangerous, I'll tell you to put them on. The weather today is good, a slight breeze of between four and six Knots, so there are no rough seas, and we're not expecting any trouble.' He paused. 'Unless one of you causes trouble.' He smiled at them. Squalls can blow up at any time of year, but we not expecting any.

'The VHF radio is over here so we can call ashore, or SOS if necessary. Has anyone used one of these before?'

A hand went up, and a student named Jonathan said, 'Yes, I have, on my dad's boat in Plymouth harbour. We moor it by the Mount on the Plym.'

'Great,' said Juan. 'Without understanding any of what Jonathan had said. 'You can use it today. When we take samples, you can log our position.'

'Finally, for safe keeping, I'd advise that you all put any electrical or battery devices in a bag so we can store them away from the sea water. They just don't mix, and you don't want to lose your phone when you are so far from home.'

Everyone duly handed their phones to Juan, who placed them in a plastic zip-lock bag, and left them in a slight hollow in the central table.

'Right, off we go then,' Juan cheerfully announced. 'Please take your seats around the hulls, either side or upstairs on the saloon roof or even on the netting area.'

He left for the cockpit, where he started the engines. They sputtered into life and idled. Juan then shouted instructions to the marina assistants in the shallows, who let go of the ropes holding the catamaran steady and pushed it away from the shore. Students gathered up the lines and left them in a neat pile on either hull, near the steps.

Juan engaged the gears, and the catamaran edged away from the beach, through the small breaking waves, out towards the open sea.

Soon they were travelling at what felt like fifty miles per hour, but was in fact a much slower, six knots against a strong onshore sea breeze.

Jane found it exhilarating. Everyone was smiling, and a small group had established themselves on the netted area, lying with their faces pushed against the netting, feeling the wind and occasional splashes of beautiful clear aquamarine seawater that made them squeal with laughter.

Several miles out they slowed, and Juan cut the engines. The catamaran bobbed in the light ocean swell. Juan announced that they would take some samples and then put the mainsail up.

Each student was given a bag and a log sheet to record time of day and co-ordinates. In each bag was a plastic twenty-millilitre screw-cap specimen jar. Jonathan shouted out the coordinates: forty-three degrees thirty-eight minutes north, one hundred and thirteen degrees and fourteen minutes west. The students duly recorded the details on their log sheet and then stepped down via steps on the hull to take a sample of the ocean water.

'Once you've taken your samples, put them in the bag and label them and place them in the cool-box here.' By his feet lay a blue and white cool-box, formerly belonging to a family, where it once held cool drinks and treats for a day out; now contained bags with ocean water samples. 'It keeps the samples out of the sun and prevents them rolling around the floor,' Juan instructed.

Once all the samples had been taken, Juan organised some students to assist with the winching of the mainsail, and to provide space for the boom to swing around safely.

Once up, the sail made a startling transformation, from a limp, loose sheet flapping in a breeze, to a rigid aerofoil sail, merely with the tightening of the uphaul rope.

The boat headed off, in almost complete silence, but for the splashing of the waves against the hulls, as they cut their way through the sea.

Soon they were accompanied by a pod of dolphins. Eight of them crossed the bow waves and shot under the boat's hulls. The students stood and watched and pointed at them, calling and whistling to get another glimpse of then. After ten minutes or so the dolphins left as quickly as they had appeared.

For several hours the students sailed, stopped and ate lunch, took more samples and swam. Jonathan excelled at showing some of the students the charts and how to plot their position. Some students sat around and were taught how to make knots with their shoelaces, and other bits of rope and string. They tried to tie "sheepshank", "halyard", and "reef" knots, and their collective favourite, the "bowline", which they used to tie fenders to the lifeline cable that run around the boat.

By late afternoon Juan could sense the students were becoming tired; they had been busy and excited most of the day. They appeared to be waning slightly, so he decided it was time to head back to shore.

Under the power of mainsail, they changed direction and saw another pod of dolphins; heading towards them and followed them for a while. The group were again excited, and their spirits lifted.

As they followed, they suddenly entered into a dense patch of sea mist. Soon they were completely engulfed. 'Mosmanu,' Juan muttered. He didn't know exactly where they were. He checked the GPS and saw they were only nine miles offshore. However, they hadn't seen another boat all day, and there was nothing on the charts they should be concerned about. Juan continued on, expecting to come out the other side of the sea mist instantly, but it became thicker and denser. Soon the light was restricted, and Juan reefed the mainsail a little to slow the boat. They all started to taste and smell something very unnatural, it caused their eyes to blink and water. A couple of the group began to cough, and the water looked different.

'It looks like we've hit upon an algae-type bloom,' Juan said. The water looked red, viscous and thick. It had flecks of white foam. 'I'm not sure what type of red algae this is though,' Juan commented, 'but some can be harmful, so we'll use gloves when we sample this.'

The mist above thinned slightly, and a little light broke through. They were all shocked by what lay before them; the sea looked deep red, like blood, with a broken white foam layer and with all types of plastic waste broken through the surface. There were carcasses of fish and birds and several turtles and dolphins, at different stages of decomposition. Some were caught in the plastic flotsam and nets. The view was shocking. 'My god, what is this?' Juan muttered under his breath. In his eight years at the university and in all his sailing he had never witnessed such a sight.

The boat continued to glide silently through the turgid red sea at about four knots, occasionally passing through some patches of dense, acrid smells, and the boat's hull bumped along debris just below the surface. The mist closed in and again the light was blocked out. Juan realised they had been travelling west and decided to head south to break out of this toxic area.

Juan announced that they would tack; he got all the crew to be ready to come about. The wind was light, and he started the engines. 'Coming about,' Juan shouted, and the boat quietly turned to the south. As they straightened up something underwater struck the hulls. The starboard hull shook and made a deep grating sound as it rose over the obstruction in the water. Three students sitting on the edge of the deck fell backwards into the water, and others fell into the net between the hulls. The motors continued, but now with the starboard hull propellers clear of the water, they spun splashing water and debris over the deck and students. The sudden stop had caused everything to slide off the surfaces of the boat. Cups, bottles and bags had fallen onto the floor and lay in disorderly heaps on the port hull floor.

Juan stumbled to the cockpit to shut off the engines. 'Roll call, everyone.' Juan shouted all their names.

'Jonathan?'

'I'm here with Liz,' Jonathan responded from behind Juan.

'Jane?'

'I'm over here,' Jane shouted from the netting area; she had been knocked off the starboard hull into the net.

'Emily?' There was no response.

'Emily?'

'She's here with me,' Jo shouted. Emily was sitting on an upturned hull of a smaller boat next to the catamaran with Jo. Both had been thrown off the hull onto this upturned boat, just missing the water. Juan moved uphill across the catamaran, to see where they had been thrown. Through the dense mist, he could see them sitting on the hull, about five metres away. 'Just stay there, guys, let me check on the others.'

Juan clambered back to the saloon. 'Where are you, Lloyd and Jodie?' Juan shouted.

'Jodie and me are below deck in the galley,' Lloyd responded.

Returning to Jo and Emily, Juan could see that they were at sea level, below the bow of the starboard hull, which was now two metres out of the water. Juan reached for the neat pile of rope and called Jo.

'Can you catch this, Jo? I'm throwing you a line; I'll pull you to the stern of the hull.'

'Oh, okay,' replied Jo. 'I'm ready.'

On the third attempt, Jo caught the line, and Juan slowly pulled Jo and Emily over. On each pull, the viscous, red seawater lapped up the sides of the upturned hull. Bubbles emerging around the hull suggested that not all was well with the buoyancy of the craft; Juan increased his effort with a sense of urgency. As they approached the starboard Hull, Emily jumped towards the steps, two metres away. Juan caught her arm, but her legs went into the water; Emily somehow managed to plant her feet on the lowest, submerged step. She climbed up the steps towards Juan. 'Oh, thank you, Juan!' she cried and hugged him.

'Juan, look!' Jo said, pointing to the hull he was standing on. Bubbles emerged around the hull's edges; it was starting to roll over.

'Jo, quick! Jump!' Juan ordered.

Jo made a huge leap, causing the hull to roll over and begin to sink. Jo landed with both feet on the bottom step, just under the water. The hull he had just jumped from continued to bubble and sank below the surface.

Everyone was now on board, and Juan knew he needed to get everyone central in the boat to try and get the boat level.

'Everyone get mid-ships, to the saloon. I'm going to try and push us off. Everyone off the starboard hull.'

The students moved from the net and each hull into the central cabin.

Juan moved up to the bow of the starboard hull, two metres above the watermark, and leaned over the bow. He could see a huge mass of congealed plastic just under the reddish foam on the surface of the water. He sat on the side of the hull and kicked away at the plastic.

It barely moved. Juan kicked and kicked again with more effort. The water splashed him, and his eyes began to feel sore.

The kicks started to have some effect; the plastic and debris began to part, and the hull dropped slightly. He kicked at the newly surfaced plastic, and that too parted. It rolled in the water, away from the hull; more plastic parted further along the hull, and it dropped further. The propellers made contact with the surface of the water.

Juan was almost exhausted. He leant over to pull out a mass of plastic and netting. As he strained to pull up the snagged debris, it suddenly gave way, to reveal a partially dissolved body. The face and head were bleached and hairless, and the eyes were hollow sockets. Juan screamed and let go, and scrambled back onto the hull deck. He looked back down and could see the body bobbing on the surface; it was surrounded by red, foam-streaked water and debris, the mouth gaping, and staring at him through hollow eyes. The image would haunt him for years to come.

Juan stood in stunned silence; he was tired, his eyes stung, and his arms and legs ached. Jonathan came forwards to support him. 'Come and sit down, Juan. Come and rest.'

The starboard hull was now level in the water, with the propellers a metre below the surface. But the boat continued to list towards the port hull. 'Why is the port hull lower?' Juan asked.

Jonathan went to look; he passed the other students in the saloon, seated on the curved seating area.

All the students were complaining of sore skin and stinging eyes. They were beginning to get scared.

Jonathan got to the port hull and was shocked to see the sample box, the seat cushions, shoes, jackets, and backpacks were all just flotsam in the pool at the bottom of the port hull.

'Shit!' He stumbled uphill, quickly, back to Juan.

'There's about a metre of water in the port hull, Juan. What should we do?'

'Jonathan, go and start the engines, get the bilge pumps running to drain the hull. We can motor away as the hull is draining.' Jonathan nodded. 'You need to do this, I can barely feel my hands,' Juan added. Jonathan looked down to see Juan's hands heavily blistered. In the dim light, he could just see that Juan's eyes were swollen and almost closed. Jonathan's legs were also hurting, but nothing like Juan's.

'Sure, but let's get you into the Saloon,' Jonathan said, and helped Juan inside. Emily came out to assist as he approached the cabin. 'Take care of him. I'll start the engines.'

Jonathan switched on the ignition and primed the motors. On a single turn of the key, both engines roared into action. He let them idle and then switched on the bilge pumps. The unmistakable deep thud of the powerful bilge pumps kicked in.

Jonathan went back to the helm, pushed the gear to reverse. The boat strained to reverse; he applied more power, then more, and the craft freed itself with a jolt. Jonathan pushed the gears back into idle and then forward, and turned the helm to port. The boat started to move through the viscous red sea, the reefed mainsail fluttered with the movement of the air.

The boat slowly motored away from the dense plastic and toxic area. The mist was still, and the students sat motionless in the saloon; they were coughing, and water started to ebb and flow around their ankles from the port hull.

Just minutes into the journey the bilge pumps, and then the engine, spluttered and died. Steam came out of the engine compartment. Jonathan made several futile attempts to start the engine, but it was dead.

Jonathan opened the engine compartment and could see red water was running from the corrugated plastic water inlet hose. The hose appeared to have melted and was now unable to supply cooling water to the engine. The engine had overheated and was unable to start again.

'We have no engine,' Jonathan told Juan. 'It appears the water hoses are leaking. How did maintenance not spot this?'

The boat continued to heel over to port, and now the starboard hull had also begun to take on water. The whole crew were confused, and more of them were starting to wheeze and cough.

Jonathan suggested pumping the bilge pumps manually, but this also seemed futile.

'Jonathan, please get some help and unstrap and launch the life raft. Before you inflate it, tether it to the mooring line, and cast it over the port side of the boat. Get someone to get the life jackets and flares.' Jonathan became aware that the light was fading, and he had lost all idea of time.

Jonathan and Emily unstrapped the raft, tied the mooring line, pushed it into the water and pulled the inflation line. It slowly inflated, and an orange hexagonal tent built within the raft now bobbed beside the boat. A light flashed on top of the newly inflated craft. Lloyd had recovered the life jackets and piled then on the saloon roof. He went back to bring the flares up to the deck.

Juan thanked them for working so well as a team, and asked Johnathen to try the radio. Although both hulls were filling with water there was still time to broadcast their location before they needed to get into the raft, but the water below deck had now covered the batteries within the seating area, and all power was lost. Jonathan couldn't even hear static on the radio.

While Jonathan was attempting to use the radio, Jane tried to recover some of the items floating in the hulls. She reached over for the cool-box, managing to hook the handle with a coat hanger and then pulled it out. It was much heavier than it should have been, and as she hauled it out, water streamed out from a large hole near the base.

'Look!' Jane shouted when she noticed the water pouring out. On opening the cool-box, she saw that the plastic vials had melted and a pungent red mass was evident at the base of the cool-box.

'What the fuck?' Jo exclaimed.

On deck, Emily noticed that the fenders hanging along each side of the forty-foot vessel now looked flaccid and limp.

The water continued to rise, and they congregated on the saloon roof, away from the water in the still, misty, silent air.

#

The crew sat in silence on the saloon roof. The boat was still listing but less so than previously. It seemed to have stabilised. They were all sore; their arms and feet were blistered, their lungs ached and rasped with every breath. As Juan looked at the survival raft, it slowly began to collapse in on itself and partially sink.

'Can someone get the bag of phones from the saloon?' Juan asked, with a hint of desperation in his voice.

Jo went below deck and looked for the zip-locked bag. 'Juan,' he shouted, 'It's not good news; look!' He carried out a partially degraded plastic bag containing the phones, half-filled with reddish water. 'Oh, no! Hell no!' Juan exclaimed. Everyone took their phones and made fevered attempts to power them.

Jane sheepishly pulled out her mobile from her shorts. 'I'm sorry,' she said, 'but I hope this can help.'

#

Jane trembled as she made an attempt to dial. Her hands were blistered and swollen. Nervous and desperate, she clumsily dropped the phone, and it bounced onto Jo's foot. She quickly retrieved it and tried again.

Jane attempted to call her dad, each time waiting for the transient signal to be strong enough and knowing she had less than 10% battery life left.

On the third attempt, it was answered. 'Dad, Dad, thank god! Oh, Dad, please help us!' she cried.

Chapter 6

Robert was shocked. It had been nearly six weeks since they last spoke, and now Jane was calling him from the other side of the world.

'What's up, are you okay?' he asked.

'Oh, Dad, our boat is sinking, the life raft is gone. And I'm scared,' she sobbed.

'Okay, honey, breathe, slow down. Where are you? Where did you leave from? Do you know your position?' He looked around the lounge for a paper and pen.

'We left from Port Bata, Equatorial Guinea, and I think we're about nine miles off the coast. What's our position?' she screamed out to the others. 'I have my dad on the line.' Jonathan quickly waded through the water below deck to the GPS position last recorded position on the charts. The radio was dead.

'We're fourteen degrees and thirty-four minutes east, twenty-one degrees five minutes north,' Jonathan shouted up.

Robert scribbled the figures down. 'What exactly happened? What happened to the boat and the raft?' Robert asked.

'Dad, I don't know, we hit something, and the boat is going under. The raft started sinking as soon as we inflated it.'

Bloody third-rate sailing club, he thought, *renting out a substandard vessel for kids to play on.* They would hear from him about this. Taking the money and putting his daughter's life at risk.

'Try and stay on the boat, keep it afloat, throw out what you don't need, keep bottled water and flares with you. Put on life jackets,' he rattled off.

Jane started repeating what he said. 'Dad says to get the flares, get stuff out from below, get bottled water and put on life jackets.' They all solemnly took a lifejacket from the pile and helped each other to buckle them on.

'Okay, we've done what you said, Dad.'

'Jane,' He paused. 'Tell me, is it a catamaran or a mono-hull?'

'What?' she replied.

'Has it two hulls or one?' he repeated.

'Err, two,' she replied.

'Ah, good,' Robert replied.

'Why is that important?' she asked.

'Well, the boat shouldn't roll over as it sinks, so you should be okay on top. Put your flares and fresh water on the saloon roof and light the flares when you hear something nearby.

'Honey, listen,' he said. 'I think you should turn your phone off to save the battery. Turn it on again every hour on the hour for five minutes, so we know when to call you.'

'Okay, Dad,' she sobbed. 'Don't go.'

'I'll call you back, honey, you'll be okay. I'll make some phone calls, and call back.'

'Bye, honey, take care. Be brave. Love you.' It pained him to put the phone down, but he had to try and help.

'Bye, Daddy,' she sobbed.

Robert paused as he digested his thoughts and tried to work out a plan of action.

He hadn't asked Jane about any injuries, how many people were with her, what the weather was like, anything. Should he call back? Had he given them the right advice?

Robert googled the Port Bata, Equatorial Guinea coast guard. He couldn't find a number, but he located information on vessel tracking of commercial ships and maritime news and weather for the west coast of Africa. The weather looked calm, and no storms were forecast. But he couldn't find a contact for the coast guard.

Lucy was working in Lagos. But how far away would that be from Jane? Robert had no idea of the geography of the area. But he knew that Lucy would be closer than he was.

Chapter 7

'Lucy, it's Robert.'

'Hello, you're keen, I was going to ring you later,' she answered coyly, looking out of her office window.

'No, Lucy,' he cut in abruptly. 'It's an emergency. It's Jane. She's at sea somewhere on a catamaran, and they're stranded.'

'What?' Lucy cried 'What's happened, Robert? You're scaring me.'

'Lucy, her… her boat is sinking. We've got to help her. I've gone online and tried to find the local coast guard, but I can't find anything.'

'Oh Christ, Robert. When did she ring you?' Lucy sobbed, a part of her wondering why Jane hadn't called her. But she shook off the negative thoughts, a little ashamed to be thinking like that at such a time.

'Only about ten minutes ago,' he replied. 'They are somewhere near Port Bata in Equatorial Guinea.'

She pondered slightly then quickly replied, 'I have some recruitment contacts in that area. They get recruits for the petrochemicals refineries around that port. I'll ask someone to give me the contacts for the coast guard, or harbour master, or police, or bloody someone, anyone!'

'Robert, let me get off the line now. Don't worry, let's pray that we can get to our little girl. I'll make some calls and let you know.'

'Okay, darling. Bye.'

Lucy ended the call, and then quickly rang her contact in HR.

'Hello, Isabelle, it's Lucy here; can you email me any recruitment manager contacts we have in Equatorial Guinea please, near port Bata?'

'There is one main one in the area, he had thirty-two recruits this month, you want all of them as well?'

'No just the manager please.'

Isabelle replied with precision and clarity. 'The recruitment manager in Port Bata is Bill Kendry, all thirty-two recruits are for Butler Oil & Gas. I'd like to see his commission this month,' she laughed.

'Thank you, Isabelle, please email me Bill's contact details. I urgently need to contact him.'

'Sure, Lucy. It sounds urgent, is there anything else I can help with.'

'Thank you, Isabelle. Our daughter Jane is in trouble off the coast of Port Bata, I'm trying to get details for coast guard or Police there.'

'Oh dear, I do wish you luck. But Bill should be your man he knows the area well, I'll pray for your daughter. Take care, Lucy.'

Thank you, Isabelle. I appreciate that. Bye'

Lucy had heard rumours of some recruitment managers working on the fringes of the law and morality, and Bill's name had been mentioned. To address the appetite of the Oil and Gas recruitment in a booming area, some allegations of coach loads of unskilled labourers and migrants from the centre of Equatorial Guinea and some neighbouring countries has been circulating. There were also allegations of trafficking, and subsequently, an investigation was required, but now was not the time. Within a minute the details had arrived at Lucy's terminal; she found Bill's contact details and rang him.

'Hello, Bill here.'

'Hello Bill, it's Lucy Howdon at HR, Lagos.'

'Hello, Lucy.' *Lucy Howdon,* he thought. *Right here it starts, the new broom has started her enquiry.* 'How can I help you?'

'Bill, I need your help. My daughter is adrift at sea off the coast of Port Bata, and we can't find anyone to contact. Could you please contact the police and coastguard to inform them?'

Relieved and taking a breath he gasped, 'Oh yes, yes of course. Err there is a coast guard at Malabo, I'll try now. Can you send me a text or email the details? You know, the name of the boat, position or whatever you have to help.' Lucy had noted Bill's intake of breath.

'Yes, of course, Bill. I'm leaving for the airport now to get there, but I'll text on the way.'

'Thanks, Bill,' she added.

'No problem, Lucy. Let me see what I can do.'

Lucy and Bill hung up. Lucy quickly texted Robert to forward the position and boat details to her. She picked up her jacket and handbag. She needed to get straight to the airport.

#

As Lucy stood waiting at the departure gate, she texted Bill the details Robert had sent, and then rang Robert to give him a heads up on the progress.

'Robert, I have a flight leaving in ten minutes. I'll be at Port Bata within three hours.'

'Ah, that's good, I'm also on the way to Heathrow airport. The next flight's not for two hours, so I probably won't be there until after 8 pm. I'm afraid there are no connections I can take to speed this up.'

Lucy interrupted him. 'Rob, I've just got a text from Bill; thanks for the details, they have dispatched the coast guard, Bill says he will keep me posted. Thank god!'

'Well, that's something, at least. Well done you!'

'Not me, Rob, thanks to Bill, and you, darling. Let's keep our fingers crossed.'

'Lucy, can you call Jane before you fly down? I said we'd call on the hour, to tell her someone is on their way.'

'Oh, Robert.' Lucy paused.

'Lucy, you still there?' Robert asked.

'Oh Robert, I'm not sure I can talk to her right now. I, I don't know if I can...' Lucy started to sob, her usual controlled demeanour buckling at the thought of her daughter suffering.

'No problem, love, I'll call. You catch your flight, I'll do it now. Love you.' Robert kissed the phone.

'Oh Robert, I'm sorry, thank you,' she sobbed.

At the last moment before take-off, while belted and waiting for the aircraft to taxi, Lucy tried to call Jane. But her timing was off; it wasn't on the hour. On each of three attempts, Lucy couldn't get through to Jane's phone. A stern stewardess asked twice that Lucy turn her phone off. Eventually, Lucy complied, but she worried all the way to Port Bata, fretting and making herself tearful, remembering Jane as a child, and moments throughout her life. Lucy quietly sobbed, looking at photos of Jane, and her family on her mobile. This was the worst flight she had ever taken.

#

A fresh onshore breeze slowly drifted the boat into clear coastal waters; away from the toxic island and the lethal red sludge. The night was dark, and a starless sky masked the catamaran in the featureless ocean. The catamaran was partially submerged. One hull was almost wholly below water, and the other was just proud of the surface. All the crew lay motionless on the roof of the saloon.

Chapter 8

Shortly before Lucy arrived at Port Bata airport, and four hours after the harbour master was initially alerted. the patrol boat edged towards a dark mass drifting ahead of them. A powerful spotlight fixed to the bow of the patrol boat, scanned the horizon back and forth searching for the catamaran as it slowly headed further out to sea.

Ahead, off the starboard bow, the coastguard crew suddenly made out the mast of the catamaran. As they slowly approached the catamaran, the spotlight illuminated the actual condition of the boat. It looked beaten; it was pitted and stained, the fenders were deflated, and a partially submerged orange life raft floated limply, tethered to the damaged port hull. The scene was lifeless apart from the occasional movement of the sail in the breeze. Closer they could see bodies lying on the catamaran. Towels were placed over their heads.

The catamaran crew were motionless, apart for the occasional cough and wheeze. Towels which had been doused in water from the bottles lay over their faces to ease the stinging of their eyes, and now they also offered protection from the stiffening breeze.

Juan was aware of some noise. Was it a boat? Help? He started to move, trying to reach for a flare when he saw the light from the Patrol boat shine on him. He winced at the intense light and fell back, again wincing in pain.

There was neither joy nor excitement from the catamaran team as the rescue boat crew boarded and started to give first aid, and help them to their feet. Some students were able to stand, and others were assisted into the patrol boat; some had to be carried. Juan struggled slowly to his feet unaided; he helped Jane to her feet, and then the patrol boat crew came forward to take over. Juan made his own way onto the patrol boat, clambering along the angled, slippery deck to the water's edge.

They gathered on the patrol boat, solemn and exhausted. The Coast Guard skipper brought the mainsail down and tied the catamaran to the stern of the patrol boat. The wrecked boat was slowly towed back to Port Bata.

#

An ambulance greeted the Patrol Boat on arrival at Port Bata. The blue lights flashed in the dark night, and Paramedics wrapped the crew in foil blankets and gave them bottles of water, as they were assisted off of the Patrol Boat. At Port Bata Hospital, they all sat quietly in an anteroom until the doctor brought each one in to be checked and given treatment. Their blistered eyes and skin were washed with sterile distilled water and dried carefully, in order not to break the skin. Apart from sores eyes, blistering and sore throats, there appeared to be no serious damage. Juan's blistering was the most severe, especially around his ankles and his arms, and there was a lot of broken skin on his hands and knuckles.

'Juan, what did this,' the doctor asked.

'Just water, red water,' Juan replied.

'This is not caused by water,' Turning to a nurse, the doctor muttered, 'These are blisters caused by chemical reactions; possibly a solvent judging by the smell, wash them in sterile water and cover them with a sterile gauze soaked in water. He may need some antiseptic cream later.

'Sir, are you in pain?' Asked the nurse.

'A little,' Juan replied.

The nurse gave him some tablets and a plastic cup of water.

'Take these; they will help.'

Juan's broken skin was washed and smeared with antiseptic cream and bandaged. Each of the students was provided with a hospital bed so they could get some sleep and recover.

The onshore wind that gently blew the catamaran away from what they had thought was just a red algae bloom, had probably saved their lives.

#

Lucy arrived at Bata International Airport and took the twenty-minute taxi trip to the Ibis Hotel at Bata. The pleasant but basic hotel overlooked the palm tree-lined beach; but Lucy had booked it for its close proximity to the town centre and the hospital, not the view. Lucy attempted to call Robert, but there was no answer. And she suspected he was on silent mode during his flight.

Once she had checked in, she asked at reception for a taxi to the hospital. One was immediately available, and she got there in under five minutes. At the hospital, Lucy asked at reception for the young crew that had been brought in, and she was directed to the lower block; a mixed ward at the front of the building. Lucy thanked the staff and headed down the stairs. She passed through double doors and found herself in the Ward. Lucy saw some of the crew asleep. Their faces look reddened and bloated, and their breathing rasped slightly. Then she saw Jane lying asleep. Lucy cried quietly, seeing her daughter lying there. She wanted to run over and scoop Jane up in her arms, but couldn't wake her. Lucy sat down next to the bed sobbing quietly. Her maternal instincts kicked in and her emotions ruled, it was a painful blend of relief and guilt. A ward nurse walked past and came over to Lucy.

'Are you ok my dear?' she asked.

'Ohh yes, yes thank you,' Lucy replied drying her eyes.

'It's my daughter. I'm so relieved she is here.'

'There is no lasting damage, my dear, she will heal fine.'

She noticed the relief in Lucy's face and added 'Take your time my dear, I'll leave you here, but come and find me if you need anything.'

'Thank you.'

The nurse walked away, and Lucy sat for a while holding Jane's bandaged hand, thankful that there was no lasting damage and so grateful Jane was here at all.

Lucy nodded off to sleep on several occasions and woke up suddenly, straightening herself up jerkily. Seeing Jane was still asleep, and that an hour had passed, she thought it was time to leave. She kissed Jane's reddened forehead and went back to reception.

'Excuse me,' Lucy said to the woman at reception who had directed her on her arrival. 'My daughter and her friends in there, do you know what happened to them?'

'There's nothing to worry about, senora.' The nurse smiled. 'It's only blistering, some sun damage and a little dehydration.'

'Blisters?' said Lucy. 'What caused them?'

'Well, the doctor thinks this skin damage was caused by some chemical.'

'Chemical? Was this at sea? How is that possible?'

'Yes, at sea.' The nurse shrugged. 'It is quite unusual, I agree, but we've seen it before.'

'Before? When?' asked Lucy.

'Several months ago; some fishermen were picked up with similar blisters.'

'Really? How on earth could this happen?'

The nurse shrugged, and Lucy could feel herself getting emotional again, thinking how close she had come to losing Jane.

'Thank you, thank you for your time,' she said, her voice husky with suppressed tears.

'You're welcome, senora. Good night.'

'Good night,' Lucy replied as she walked out into the warm dawn air.

Dawn was starting to break, and in the quietness of the morning Lucy decided to walk back to the hotel. It was a surprisingly short walk, and she continued to the beach and harbour. In the early light, she stood to watch fishing boats heading out to sea, silhouetted against the early sun. Walking towards the marina, near the pontoon Lucy noticed a mast that emerged from below the water line. Stepping closer, she could make out a catamaran, one hull a metre below the surface of the water and the other hull barely breaking the surface. She could also make out a gash in the submerged starboard bow; as she got closer, she could see the resin matrices around the gash, where the upper gel coat skin was missing. It was stained a reddish colour. All the fenders were deflated and hung limply along the side of the boat. A pile of orange plastic and nylon was thrown on the back of the boat

Walking further along the pontoon, Lucy noticed a single flat-bottomed boat. It was also partially submerged, and it had a red, stained floor. The only identifying feature was a corncob logo stamped on the right of the screen.

Lucy thought no more of it and headed back to the hotel.

As she approached the hotel, Lucy dialled Robert from her mobile and waited for an answer. It picked up immediately.

'Robert, where are you?'

'I'm in our room; where are you?' he replied.

'Thank god you're here. I'm coming into the reception.'

'I'll be right down,' he replied and hung up.

Robert soon arrived in the reception area and kissed Lucy and gave her a big hug. Lucy was glad to see him and held him tight.

'You've seen our little girl?' he whispered.

'Yes, she's safe and well. Oh, Robert, we almost lost her.' She started to sob again.

'Now, now,' Robert said soothingly. 'We're with her now, let's be strong for her.'

Lucy agreed and wiped her eyes. 'Let's both go and see her.'

'No, we can't,' he said. 'When I rang, they said she was sleeping.'

'Yes, she was, but they allowed me in. Who said no?' asked Lucy?

'The main medic,' he replied.

'There were none when I left,' Lucy said, looking confused.

'Really? Come on then, let's go back.' They turned and headed out of the hotel.

When they arrived at the hospital, there were indeed medics. They were wearing white laboratory coats, facemasks and gloves and moved with some urgency, armed with swabs and sample bags. The staff Lucy spoke to earlier had all disappeared.

'This area is restricted!' A woman further down the corridor shouted at them from behind a mask.

'I'm here to see my daughter.'

'Sorry, senora, this area is restricted until we determine the cause of the outbreak.'

'What outbreak?' Lucy looked at Robert, confused. 'There's no outbreak, it was an accident; they are fine.'

'Senora, I beg to differ.' A tall man in a lab coat stepped forward. He was eloquent, confident and polite, and carried the air of authority. 'Could I ask that you go no further? We need to quarantine this area until we can be sure there is no contagion.'

'But I was in here earlier, the nurses never mentioned contagion then.'

'Well, it should all be straightforward, then; I suggest you return later today, senora. We can't be too sure; we need to check to be on the safe side.'

Lucy noticed the logo on his lab coat; it was the same as the one she had seen on the flat-bottomed boat.

'What was her name? Your daughter's name? We'll tell her you were here and that she can contact you.'

Lucy looked at Robert, confused. 'Yes. Yes of course. Her name is Jane, Jane Howdon. I'm Lucy Howdon, and this is my husband, Robert, her father.'

The stranger smiled and looked at them both. 'And where are you staying?' he asked and quickly added, 'She can use a phone to call you there.'

'We are at the Bata Hilton, room 426.' Relieved that Jane was being looked after, and she could call, Lucy was happy to retire back to the hotel. She could see that the medical caution was necessary, but she didn't understand why it was only happening now, and not earlier.

The stranger looked at Robert directly and smiled. 'I won't keep you. Is it okay if you see yourselves out?'

'Good night,' he added. He watched them walk down the corridor and took off his latex gloves, revealing a silver cygnet ring on his left index finger.

Lucy and Robert walked back to the hotel along the main road, past the local shops and the ever-present palm trees. It was still early; just after dawn and quiet. The normal hustle and bustle of the town was yet to begin. The gnawing worry that Lucy thought had passed came to the surface again. She struggled to contain her emotions.

Chapter 9

News had somehow spread that Robert Howdon was in town and his daughter had been in an accident. Two local news reporters and a TV camera had taken up residence in the hotel lobby. Lucy was at a table, talking on the phone to Jane, watching the reporters stopping passers-by in the hotel reception area and asking them questions.

Robert arrived in the reception lobby. He saw Lucy in the breakfast room headed across to her table.

Suddenly a reporter stepped in front of him.

'Mr Howdon. Can you tell us anything about your daughter's rescue? Mr Howdon, were you involved? How is she, Mr Howdon?'

'Oh, she's good, thank you. No, no comment, thank you.' Robert did his best to escape the reporter. However, two other reporters waiting at reception saw the interaction and also headed over.

'Mr Howdon, is this publicity for your book? Is it a hoax?' The first reporter asked.

'What? No, of course, it isn't. I'm relieved and happy. My daughter is safe and well.' A couple of camera flashes went off.

'Now, if you don't mind, I want to have my breakfast.' But the reporters didn't stop.

'Is this a hoax, are you trying to get publicity, Mr Howdon?'

Lucy looked over at him. They exchanged concerned glances. Robert realised he shouldn't head over to Lucy or get her involved, as she would also be hounded, so he backed away to the door leading to the dining room and then onto the garden.

Robert left the hotel grounds and headed into town; the reporters only followed for two blocks or so. Once he was clear of them, he changed direction and headed for the harbour.

He walked towards the marina and looked for the boat that Lucy had told him about, but it wasn't there, and neither was the catamaran. However, walking the length of the harbour wall, he saw red streaked water and a blood-like smear along the harbour wall. He shuddered.

Robert took his phone and went back to the coast guard website he found when he had googled for the coast guard the day before. He then looked at the menu and selected the tracking option. He looked at boat movements that morning; all registered boats were listed. Each vessel had a time logged on arrival and at departure by GPS tracking. He saw two boats had left at seven the previous morning, registered to GM Agro-Tech.

He took a note of the boats' IDs and looked through the online journal for the last month, and then three months. He saw that during the last month there were trips each night from the harbour with these ID's, but before that these boats had only been making a night-time journey once a week.

Why? How does this all add up? he thought.

Robert carried on walking and saw the harbour master's office. He felt an urge to meet the harbour master and shake his hand and thank him for saving his daughter. Hearing laughter from the office, he smiled.

As Robert passed the harbour master's office, he glanced through the window, he was surprised to see Professor Wilmsford, laughing with the harbour master, and shaking his hand. Robert was about to call up to him and walk into the office to greet him but had second thoughts.

What is The Prof doing here? Robert paused for thought and looked back again to see The Prof handing a package over to the harbour master. They shook hands and laughed again. The harbour master kissed both of The Prof's cheeks and patted him on the back as he turned to leave. 'Adios, amigo mio.'

'Adios, and don't forget a red Algae bloom if they ask,' The Prof smiled as he left the building.

'Si, Si,' the harbour master called out laughing.

Robert walked behind some bushes adjacent to the port car park and waited for The Prof to pass. He sauntered by, oblivious to Robert's presence. He looked at his phone and then held it to his ear.

'Yes, it's done, there shouldn't be any more about the incident. The press hasn't been here yet, but we're ready,' he smiled and added, 'catch you later; take care, pal,' and carried on walking to the harbour pontoon. When he approached the water, he reached into his pocket and took out a small bunch of keys. He dropped them into the water and headed towards the north end of the car park. Robert, still observing, walked over to the water and looked down into the water where the keys had been dropped.

Just a metre below the surface was a sunken, flat-bottomed boat. Through the clear but tainted water, Robert could see the keys had dropped behind the pilot seat onto the floor, which was tinged with a reddish stain.

Robert's eyes darted around the boat looking for some identifying marks. On the inside of the windshield above the dashboard there was a small disc with a corncob logo. Below it was a registration number. Robert looked at his tracking numbers from the coastguard website on his phone, and saw that one matched this number under the logo. Robert looked back towards The Prof; he could still see him in his white t-shirt with chino shorts and blue deck shoes, blithely walking away.

#

Robert called Jane.

'How are you, my darling? You okay?'

'Hello, Daddy. Yes, I'm good. Still a little sore, but not bad really. Mum is here with me. Do you want to speak to her?'

'Where are you?' he asked.

'I'm at the hospital canteen, getting breakfast. Mum is here to pick me up. Are you coming? Shall we wait for you or shall we meet you somewhere? I heard that you got some grief from the reporters this morning.'

'I'll be there shortly; I'll come along the sea wall,' he thought this would be the best route; he could head in the side entrance and bypass reception, in case any reporters were there.

Soon Robert was with them.

'How are you, darling?' Robert asked, hugging her, and kissing her on the forehead. Lucy smiled at both of them.

'I'm good. Thank you for your help, Daddy. I think you saved us.'

'From what I heard you were lucky that the wind changed. Where did you get that bloody boat from? It was a disgrace.'

'Dad, the boat was fine, it was the sea that caused all the damage. The boat was beautiful. We saw dolphins. Oh, and some dead animals and plastics; that bit was awful.

'But you should ask Juan, the skipper; he took us through the safety stuff at the beginning… he is over there look.' Robert felt sheepish, remembering his less than generous opinion about what he thought was a substandard yacht. He reassured Jane that he would talk to Juan and thank him.

'Where are the medics?'

'They've all gone,' Jane said. 'They washed us all, took our clothes and left us with these gowns! But it's no problem, I have other clothes at the campus. My clothes stunk with that yuk on them anyway.'

Lucy and Jane started making plans to get clean clothes and bring them to the hospital for her.

Robert looked around for Juan. He was talking with a nurse. Robert walked over, and the nurse smiled at Robert and left, waving at Juan.

'Hello,' Robert said. 'I'm Jane's dad. Jane says you have really been a hero, and I wanted to thank you for your help.' Juan smiled and looked slightly embarrassed.

Robert went on. 'If it's okay, could you talk me through what happened, please?'

'Yes of course,' Juan said. 'Really, we just hit something when we were sailing, not hard, but we started to sink. We all started coughing and our eyes hurt, and we all got these blisters.' Juan showed Robert his hands, rotating them to show both sides.

Robert winced at Juan's large blisters and soreness over his arms and legs. He could see that Juan was still suffering; his eyes were puffy, and his face was red and greasy.

'Then the engine wouldn't start, and we began to capsize.'

'Juan do you have any idea what caused this?' Robert's face was etched with a mixture of intrigue and concern.

'Well, initially I thought it was an algae bloom, the water was quite red and viscous. But an algae bloom couldn't cause this damage,' Juan replied. 'Funny thing: the strong, almost sweet smell is recognisable, at a place where I've been to, further down the coast.'

'Really?' said Robert. 'Where, out at sea?'

'No sir, at a village. I've taken students there. It's deserted now. The air smells like yesterday's sea, and the ground and walls are stained just like the boats were.'

Robert's mind raced; there was a lot more to this incident than a simple accident at sea. 'And you don't know what caused that?'

'No, but the samples we took might help, maybe?'

'What samples,' asked Robert. 'No one mentioned any samples.'

'We took a lot of samples during the day, but the plastic vials all melted in the cool box. Luckily I had some samples in glass vials and I rescued them before the cool box sank.'

'They melted?' Robert was confused and alarmed, equally. 'I think you could be right; they may help. Where are they? Are they being tested? Could they help with your treatment?'

'No, they are here, they are in my back pack.' He pointed to a chair on which rested a khaki canvas backpack. Robert picked it up and handed it to Juan.

'If you don't mind, sir, could you take them out of the pocket on the right? My hands are too sore to do it.'

'Of course,' Robert replied, feeling stupid that he hadn't thought of offering. 'Here we are.' He found himself holding three glass vials in his hand. Each contained about 10 ml of thick red liquid.

'What is this?' he asked.

'Water, taken from the sea before the boat started to sink,' Juan replied.

'Water? That's incredible.' Robert looked at the turgid red contents of the vial, with a viscous, clear meniscus on the surface. He shook the small bottle and instinctively opened the lid and sniffed the liquid. 'No, don't do that!' shouted Juan.

Robert's eyes immediately stung, and the sharp, acrid fumes produced a sudden tightness in his nostrils and throat. He was stunned and unable to breathe; a gasp stayed locked in his throat, trapped by the poisonous secret held in the vial. He was caught in a state of paralysis for what seemed like minutes. Finally, he breathed in a huge gulp of air and coughed. 'Hell, what is that?' He looked down at the bottle and hurriedly put the cap back on.

'Sir, be careful, that stuff is dangerous,' Juan looked scared. 'There is acid or something in there.'

'It's certainly not pure sea water,' Robert agreed. 'God knows what that is. It had a strange, sweet, burnt pear type of smell!'

'Yes,' agreed Juan. 'That is what I smelt at sea.'

'Who will you get to analyse this?'

'I will get them done on campus, but we should keep them in a fridge, for safe keeping. Would you mind taking them, and I'll pick them up from you? But don't open them again.' He smiled.

'Of course,' said Robert. 'I'm sure I can squeeze them into the mini bar in my hotel room.' He laughed. Seeing, as if for the first time, how weary Juan was, he thought it was time to say goodbye.

'Well, thank you, Juan, for your help and for saving my daughter and the crew; you have been really brave. When you are better, I'd like you to show me the village you spoke of.'

'Of course, sir.' Juan smiled again, wearily. 'Although may I ask a favour, please?'

'Of course,' said Robert, 'What it is?'

'Can I have a signed copy of your book, please?'

'Yes, definitely,' Robert laughed. 'You might even get to be the lead character in my next one. I need a hero.' He patted Juan's shoulder and walked away out of the infirmary, clutching the vials. Juan watched him leave, and then his eyes slowly closed, and he slept.

#

In a smart modern apartment in West London, a mobile phone rang. Lorraine, entering the hall through her apartment front door, hastily put her bags down and reached into her jacket pocket for her mobile phone. 'Hello,' she answered.

'Lorraine, where are you?' the voice asked.

'Hugh? Hello, I've just arrived home, why?'

'You need to get out here now.'

'What? Now? Where are you?' Lorraine asked, trying to understand.

'If you were doing your bloody job you'd be here. Robert is here being crawled over by journalists.'

'Where's here, Hugh?'

'Port Bata, Lorraine, where do you fucking think?' We agreed that you stick to him like glue and maximise our publicity, but you're there, and he's here. What the hell were you thinking?'

'Okay, Hugh, calm down, don't overreact, I'll be there in the morning.'

'No, you fucking won't. You'll get here tonight. I'll book a room for you in the Bata Hilton, where he is staying. Get close to him and keep him away from his daughter at the hospital.

Hugh hung up, and Lorraine stared at the phone and shook her head. 'Oh my god, what did he mean? Robert's daughters are in Hospital?'

Feeling concerned, Lorraine picked up her phone and messaged Debbie to cover for her at work and asked her to feed Jessica. She then rang the airport to book her flights to Port Bata, Equatorial Guinea. Still upset at Hugh's tone, and worried about Roberts daughter, she packed a carry-on case and headed to Heathrow Airport.

#

As Robert made his way back to the hotel, he tried to tie up everything that had happened: his daughter's experience, her symptoms (and Juan's, which were worse), the confusion at the hospital, the logo on the sunken boat, nightly boat trips, the smell of that sample.

Were they connected? If they were, he couldn't see how.

At the hotel, Robert logged on to catch up with his email. As he entered his details, a cascade of twitter feeds filled the screen.

'What now?' he exclaimed. 'What's all this?'

He read a few of the tweets. It seemed that the reporters' questions that morning, suggesting he had arranged the boat incident to pump up his book sales, seemed to have struck a nerve with some of his followers, new and old.

The reporters' questions and subsequent assumptions in their published articles were just plain wrong. He had vehemently denied them. But it seemed that, regardless of what Robert had said, they had interpreted his denial as an admission of guilt.

Mr Howdon, I'm surprised you would stoop that low for publicity, I thought you were better than that.

Robert, good for you, but think of how good your sales would have been if you'd killed her.

What's your next book, you fiend? How to kill your daughter and get away with murder?

The news reports were bringing publicity for sure, but it was definitely not good publicity; Freddie must be going bananas over this. Meanwhile, #killagirl4sales was becoming a popular hashtag and going viral for all the wrong reasons.

Robert searched online through the local newspaper reports and saw an article by Fernandao Buille, already syndicated and translated into English.

This morning Mr Robert Howdon, writer of the New Horizons book, who is visiting Port Bata following his daughter's accident on Wednesday, declined to comment when he was asked about suggestions that the incident was a hoax in an attempt to boost sales of his book. The hoax appeared to have gone wrong and caused his daughter to suffer life-threatening injuries. Whilst his daughter was in critical condition and being nursed by his estranged wife, Robert Howdon has been in hiding. Adding fuel to these hoax claims, a book signing had been pre-arranged in Malabo. It has led to speculation that the hoax was an attempt to heighten the publicity and attendance at the book signing. Mr Howdon has not responded to questions and has not denied any of the claims.'

What rubbish. Where did this information come from? Why did they ignore my denials? They are just making this up. And as for a book signing, there is no book signing, what are they talking about?

He lay on his bed and reflected on all that had happened. Despite the horrible jumble of thoughts swirling around in his head, he soon drifted off into a deep sleep.

Chapter 10

The telephone rang. Robert barely stirred, but the ringing continued. He eventually woke, in darkness and fully clothed. Obviously, the efforts of the day had taken their toll, and Robert had drifted off. He glanced at the clock; it was almost seven-thirty pm. Lucy wasn't back yet.

The ringing continued, so he reluctantly rolled over and reached for the phone. 'Hello,' he said, fuzzily.

'Mr Howdon? We have a visitor for you at reception.'

'For me?' he replied. 'Who is it?'

There was a brief pause, and then the receptionist said, 'A Miss Bellamy, Lorraine Bellamy.'

'Lorraine. Lorraine? Really? I'll be right down. Thank you.'

Robert found his jacket, glanced at a mirror, tucked in his shirt and slicked back his hair. He picked up his room key and headed down to reception.

#

'Trolls,' Lorraine said, with a note of something like despair in her voice. 'They're just Trolls. You should put the record straight and confront them.' She took a sip of her wine; it tasted good and felt well deserved after her hastily arranged trip.

'But how?' Robert asked. 'Without getting into a tit for tat?'

'You mentioned a book signing. It might be a good way to settle the score.'

'Won't that just add fuel to the fire and play into their hands? Lorraine paused in thought. 'Didn't you say that there was a book signing? Have you heard anything from your agent?' Lorraine asked.

'No,' he replied. 'Nothing.' He looked at his phone. 'I could call her, but I'm sure she wouldn't have booked anything without calling me. But I'll give her a call and check it out.'

Robert called Freddie. She picked up immediately.

'Robert! For god's sake, where have you been? I've been trying to call you for the last two days.' Freddie screamed down the phone.

'I've had no calls,' he replied sheepishly. 'Why have you been trying to call me?'

'Because of Jane, of course, I wanted to know if your little girl was okay. How is she?'

'Thanks Freddie, she's better. She'll be out of hospital tomorrow.'

'That's good, honey, I'm pleased to hear that. Anyway, listen, when I heard you were off to Equatorial Guinea, I booked you a book signing at Malabo.'

'Where?'

'Malabo, The capital of Equatorial Guinea, on the island of Bioko. But don't thank me now.' Freddie was back to her ebullient self. 'You've got to get yourself there as soon as, it's only a short flight away.'

'I'm not sure,' Robert said, confused. 'When is it booked for?'

'Tomorrow afternoon, honey.'

'Well, I'm sorry. I'm still not sure this would work.'

'It would take your mind off things, honey, and anyway, Jane is getting better. But I'll understand if you want me to cancel.' Lorraine, who was beginning to get an idea of the conversation, nodded, her eyebrows raised and smiled at him.

'Hang on, Freddie.' Capping the mobile in his hand, he turned to Lorraine. 'What, what are you trying to tell me?'

'Is Freddie getting you to go on a book signing? This is the perfect opportunity to clear your name, get your side out there,' she said, also sensing an opportunity to keep Robert away from the Hospital as Hugh had requested.

'You think so?'

'Yes.'

'Okay, Freddie, can you email me the details, please.'

'That's great, honey,' she squealed. 'I'll send them right away, good luck!'

'Okay, bye.'

'Wow,' he said. 'That was intense!' He smiled at Lorraine. 'At least I know the booking was made after Jane's accident.'

'Yes, but the local press also found out after the incident, so it could still have looked like a pre-existing booking, I guess?' Lorraine said, relieved that Jane's injuries had been superficial.

'Hmm, you have a point.'

'I'll check with the service provider to see what the issue is with calls here,' Robert said thoughtfully. Several minutes later, he had contacted his ISP and gained access to the local mobile networks. Then his phone started pinging with missed calls, twitter messages and email messages. While the cacophony continued, he turned to Lorraine.

'Did I mention the samples I had?'

'No what samples do you mean?'

'They came from the water around the boat Jane was on when it started sinking. Juan, the group leader, is getting them tested on campus. Do you think you could get one tested?'

'I'm not sure what I could add,' Lorraine replied without any enthusiasm. 'There should be somewhere around here that could do it. We don't tend to test seawater samples. But if it helps, give me a sample; I could send one back to my laboratory.'

'Are you sure?' said Robert. 'That would be fantastic.'

'Yes, okay. Pass one over, and I'll send it tomorrow.'

'When I go upstairs, I'll bring one along to your room. You are staying here aren't you?'

'Yes, on the ground floor by the gardens' Lorraine replied.

He smiled; maybe they would find some answers soon. 'I'm sure Juan won't mind you testing one.'

He looked around. 'Lucy isn't back yet. I'd like to introduce her to you.'

'Er who is Lucy Robert?'

'My wife Lorraine, you have to meet, let me find out where she is. Excuse me.'

Robert stood up, pulled his mobile telephone from his pocket and walked to the window as he called Lucy.

Lorraine felt confused and a little foolish. Lorraine knew of his daughter but not of a Mrs Howdon. Perhaps she had heard but ignored this in the hope he was not attached. Why hadn't she enquired, but he didn't wear a wedding ring why would she?

95

Lorraine's was trying to think, and her attention was drawn to the TV by the bar; it was muted, but she could see that the news was on.

After displays of weather charts and some financial charts, Lorraine was surprised to see Robert's book cover appear on screen, and several images of Robert himself, taken in the same hotel. He looked distressed. She turned to him, and saw he was also facing the TV; he grimaced comically. She smiled and turned back to the TV. There was footage of the students who had been rescued. They were being treated at the hospital. They had blisters on their skin, and their faces looked sore. Some were bandaged. *Poor kids,* Lorraine mouthed silently.

Suddenly she thought she saw someone she recognised in the footage; she wasn't sure, but it looked like Hugh. She dismissed the thought. It was a fleeting shot, and it was entirely out of context. Hugh? At Port Bata hospital? What was she thinking?

The TV then showed some slightly older footage, of a fishing boat. Medics were carrying stretchers off the vessel, and laying them out on the harbour Jetty; all but one of the stretchers held body bags. The one surviving casualty was also being carried off on a stretcher. His eyes were swollen and red, and his whole face was bloated and blistered. It looked serious as if he had suffered exposure to a fire, or an acid attack.

The camera panned to the left. Behind the fishing boat, she could see a smaller, partially submerged boat, being towed by the larger fishing boat. The camera zoomed into the view, and Lorraine gasped and stood up. She recognised the logo on the boat's windscreen instantly.

Robert, who was still on the call to Lucy, pointed to the TV and said, 'Lorraine, that's the boat I saw at the harbour. Look at that logo on the windscreen.'

'See? It looks like a corn-on-the-cob.'

Lorraine nodded slowly, the implications started to sink in.

As Robert was trying to call Lucy, she appeared at reception, with a mobile, ringing loudly, buried in her leather bag.

She walked towards Robert, into the bar area, carrying several large shopping bags. Some guests sitting at their tables looked around at the commotion, and she mouthed sorry to them, becoming aware that the ringing noise was rather loud. Robert hung up, and the ringing ceased. She placed her bags on a chair next to Robert and kissed him on the cheek.

'Was that you calling me?' She smiled. 'Hello, darling, how's your day been?'

'Lucy!' Robert leaned over to kiss her. 'I've been trying to call you, where have you been?'

'I so need a drink now. Oh, everywhere! I've been walking for hours. I can safely say our daughter has fully recovered.' She laughed. 'I couldn't keep up with her in and out of the shops! I need to sit down.'

Lorraine walked towards them both and smiled. Robert took his cue and introduced them to each other. 'Lucy, this is Lorraine.'

'Lorraine?' Lucy said. 'Book signing Lorraine?'

'Ha! Yes, that's me,' Lorraine laughed. 'And a twitter user.'

'Lovely to meet you.' Lorraine straightened herself up and leaned forward on the chair to shake her hand. 'Robert told me about meeting you at the book signing. I'm so glad that someone can critique his book and his thoughts. I'm afraid that so much of this goes over my head.'

'Oh, it's easy really. It's a fascinating read.'

'What brings you here Lorraine? You're a long way from home.' Robert was struck by that; he had been so pleased to see Lorraine that he hadn't actually asked why she was there.

'Well, work mainly.'

'In Equatorial Guinea? How so?' Lucy enquired.

'Ah, well, there is a production site over here that I need to inspect, so I thought that I'd bring my trip forward when I heard about the incident.'

'Thank you, Lorraine. That's really nice of you.' Robert smiled.

'But how did you know about Jane? Was it on the news?' Lucy asked, glancing at them both.

Lorraine smiled weakly, trying to think of a convincing response. Lucy's phone rang. 'Excuse me,' she said, and then added, 'Oh, it's Jane.'

'Hello, Jane, what's up? Ah, okay. Give me twenty minutes. Yes sure. Okay, see you love you.'

'Jane said the hospital will release her tonight rather than tomorrow; she needs a lift to campus. And can we give Juan a lift too? I said yes, of course. Robert, can I have the keys, please? I'll go and pick them up.'

'Well, it's only insured in my name, perhaps I should drive. Is she ready now?'

'Yes, but are you sure you're okay to drive?' She looked at the glass tumbler in Robert's hand. 'I don't mind.'

Robert nodded, 'No problem, it's my first,' Holding the glass up and rattling the ice.

'Sorry Lorraine duty calls'

'No problem I'll need to get some sleep, it's been a long journey'

'Nice to meet you Lucy'

"and you Lorriane' Lucy replied smiling.

Lorraine and Robert picked up her bags and headed to their room.

They then walked out past reception, Robert stopped suddenly, remembering. 'Ah, hang on a second.' He dashed back to their room, leaving Lucy standing outside. As Lorraine finished her drink, Robert reappeared in the bar, clutching three glass sample tubes. He brought one over to Lorraine. 'I'd better give Juan his samples back. Here's one for you'

'Oh, thanks,' she said. 'Actually, I'm not sure what I can do with this.'

'Have a think, and I'll see you tomorrow. Are you coming to the book signing?'

'Yes, if I can,' she nodded, 'but wouldn't Lucy would rather go? I can miss it.'

'No Lucy wouldn't want to go. See you in the morning,' Robert said and went to join Lucy outside.

'I wanted to give Juan his samples back,' he explained. They headed off to pick Jane up.

Several minutes into the drive Lucy asked, 'Robert, what are your plans here?'

'Well, I'd like to get to the bottom of the injuries that Jane and the crew suffered. Something doesn't feel right. But Freddie has also arranged a book signing tomorrow. After that, I'll probably head home. What about you?' He asked.

'Now Jane is out of hospital and going back to campus, I think I'll head back to Lagos,' Lucy replied. 'I'll still be close enough to get back quickly if necessary. Jane doesn't want me hanging around.' She paused. 'But Robert, if you are staying longer, take care.'

'What do you mean?' asked Robert.

She thought about how to phrase the response. 'Well, Lorraine is pretty and clever, but I don't really trust her.'

Robert looked surprised. He glanced at Lucy and then back to the road. 'You don't trust her? Why not?'

'You heard her say that she had business here, right? What business? Why didn't she tell you straight off; and how did she find out about Jane being here?'

'She did explain,' Robert laughed in disbelief. 'She has business here, and she brought her trip forward. Why does it matter how she knew about Jane? She may have picked it up from the twitter feed, or maybe news from here got back to London.'

'And she just happens to be staying at the same hotel that we're in? That's a bit *too* coincidental, don't you think?'

'News will travel; I have got some celebrity status, you know.'

'Really!' Lucy laughed. 'Mr Celebrity. Listen to you.'

They both laughed. A few minutes later they arrived at the hospital. They pulled up at the entrance to the accident ward. Jane and Juan were standing there waiting.

They all greeted each other and piled bags into the boot before everyone got in the car. Jane and Lucy sat in the back, and Juan sat in the front passenger seat.

'Juan,' said Robert, 'I have your samples here in case you wanted them. I'll be travelling tomorrow and probably won't see you for a while.'

Juan, wearing a pair of thin, purple, sterile plastic gloves, took the samples from him. 'Thank you, sir. I will analyse these when I get back to campus.'

'Your hands look better, Juan,' Robert commented.

'My hands are healing. They gave me these sterile antiseptic gloves rather than bandages so I can return to work.'

The puffiness and redness around Juan's eyes and face were also less pronounced, and he looked far less weary.

'Well, don't rush into any work when you get back, you still need to recover fully. And enjoy being a hero while it lasts,' Robert laughed.

'No, it wasn't just me. All the students helped; Jonathan, Emily, Jane, Jo, all of them. Jonathan got the engines and bilge pumps going, and also gave the location to Jane when she was on the phone.'

'Yes, that's true, Daddy.'

'I didn't meet him. You'll have to point him out. But how are you feeling, Jane?'

'Oh, I'm much better now, thanks, dad. Although it was all a bit of a scare.'

'Well, I certainly think your shopping trip with Mum testifies to your recovery,' Robert said, trying to lighten the mood.

He drove on, while Lucy and Jane chatted in the back seat. 'And I'll be flying back later tonight, darling,' Lucy said, holding her daughter's hand.

Jane turned and hugged Lucy tight. 'Mum, thank you so much for coming, and looking after me. It was lovely to see you both.'

'I'm always at the end of the phone, and I can get here if you need me,' Lucy said.

'Thanks, Mum, I know you are. You're always there for me.'

They hugged again.

Jane seemed older, thought Robert, as if the experience had matured her, made her more of a woman and more able to look after herself.

Soon they had arrived at the campus.

Chapter 11

Breakfast at the hotel was peaceful. The management had restricted access for non-residents; although, some of the other guests eyed Robert with suspicion as he walked into the breakfast area.

Robert poured a coffee and sat near the full-length windows overlooking the garden. He enjoyed the peace, and quietly read a newspaper. Lucy had now returned to Lagos and Jane was settled back on campus; Robert had a bit of time to enjoy his own company.

Lorraine walked to breakfast from her room on the ground floor. She felt a little nervous and was unsure of the implications of what she had seen on the news, and certainly had no idea how to bring any of this up with Robert.

The book signing was late afternoon, and the flight was at midday, so they had the morning to kill. Lorraine smiled as she approached Robert, sitting at a table reading.

'Good morning Robert,' she said cheerfully as she took a seat.

'Good morning,' he replied without looking up.

'Robert, I have a little surprise for you,'

'Really, what is it?' Robert smiled as he looked up from the paper. 'When you are ready, we can take a little drive. I have something to show you.' She smiled.

'Where?' he asked.

'You'll see,' she said coyly.

#

After breakfast, they got into her little Fiat Punto hire car, which was parked outside the hotel, and headed east, towards the centre of the country. 'Lorraine, where are we going exactly?' Robert asked.

'Inland, to a production facility.' Lorraine surrendered. She continued to drive for several blocks, looking at each street sign and slowing at junctions to get her bearings.

'Do you know which way you are going?' he asked.

'Well I know it's supposed to be in this direction, but no, not really. I don't suppose it will be signposted.'

'We'll need a map then; do you have one?'

'Good point. No, but I bet they will.' Rounding a bend in the road, Lorraine spotted and headed towards a little shop buried behind piles of vegetables on stalls outside.

Robert jumped out of the car and went inside the roadside store. The shop was basically a hut with a corrugated steel front and a long, shady store inside. Wares of all types hung from the ceiling, and hundreds of other items were piled on rotary shelf units.

It was one of these rotary stands that Robert noticed a little group of maps.

He picked one up, gave the storekeeper a dollar and returned to the car.

'It's in Spanish,' Lorraine said, surprised, 'but that shouldn't be a problem.'

'Ok, so where are we heading now?' asked Robert.

'To San Carlos, up the Rio Mbini,' she replied.

Robert traced the river across the map with his finger, from Port Bata inland, and said, 'Found it. But why here?' Their destination appeared to be in the middle of nowhere, buried deep in the jungle.

'We have a production facility out here. It's where we've been sending GM bacteria to seed the digesters before we go into full production.' Lorraine handed Robert the address on a piece of paper. 'This lists all the sites that have received products from GM Agro-Tech. All the locations are Butler Oil & Gas pilot facilities. They are trying out proof of concept and production techniques, but the top two on the list are the ones that have received the most recent shipments.'

'Okay, I think I've found them.' He pointed out two spots on the map, sited reasonably close to each other.

All the production facilities were situated along the River Rio Mbini, and within a twenty-mile radius. The first two were within less than five miles distance of each other. As they headed towards the foothills, the roads became bumpy and steeper. The engine started to labour as it skidded around tight, steep bends as the jungle became more dense. Light broke through the darkness of the dense foliage periodically, causing a strobe lighting effect as they sped along. Through occasional breaks in the trees, they could see that they had climbed a long way in a relatively short distance. There were breath-taking views of the harbour and coast.

They arrived at the first site a few minutes later. The facility was locked up, and there was no discernible activity or security; in fact, it appeared to be completely unoccupied. The drive was overgrown and looked as if it hadn't been used for quite some time.

Lorraine looked out at the abandoned buildings. 'Looks like these facilities were built but never put to use. Let's move on.' They drove on; along a single track through the jungle. The car struggled with the incline and uneven terrain, throwing them both around in the car. Soon they approached the second facility on the map, just north of Maseng on the Rio Abia. This one appeared to be in full operation. The illuminated sign at the gate had the letters "B, O & G" overlaying a picture of an oil derrick, along with "in partnership with GM Agro Tech" and a corn-on-the-cob logo. Robert glanced at Lorraine; she avoided his gaze and continued to look ahead.

Although it was ten am, the dense jungle left the facility in darkness. The only light was provided by a few bright floodlights mounted on pylons and from some windows. Steam rose from the vents of a few light industrial buildings, confirming that they were active and occupied.

Lorraine continued to drive through the open gates, up to a manned barrier. Judging by the surprise on the faces of the security guards, visitors were a rare occurrence, and none were expected this morning. They looked quizzically at Lorraine's GM Agro-Tech security pass and called another guard over. He shone a torch into the car, scrutinising both occupants. He hurried off into a hut beside the barrier and picked up the phone. A few seconds later he declared 'dejarlos pasar' and moved back into the hut to activate the barrier. It lifted, and the security guards waved them through.

Lorraine turned to Robert. 'Here we are. This is my little surprise. I've brought you here to meet the production manager, Jerry. This will be the first working GM bacteria digester in the world.'

Robert smiled and looked around. The dense dark jungle surrounded a collection of new, white, single storey buildings and a larger two storey corrugated metal clad main building. The contrast between the Jungle shadows and the new building was striking. Robert was impressed. 'This looks amazing.'

He and Lorraine got out of the car, and a tall man in a fluorescent vest and a blue hard hat walked over. 'Lorraine? Lorraine Bellamy?' he asked.

'Yes. Hello, Jerry. I'm Lorraine Bellamy, and this is Robert Howdon.'

'Robert Howdon, the author?' Jerry beamed and strode over to him.

'Yes, that's me,' Robert replied.

Jerry greeted Robert warmly, shaking his hand with both hands. 'Jerry, Jerry Hawkins, I'm pleased to meet you both. I hope you enjoy your visit. If you have any questions at all, let me know.'

'Jerry, I'm so pleased you are showing me around. From what Lorraine has told me, I guess this is cutting edge technology that could change the world!'

'Absolutely!' he smiled. 'I'll be glad to show you around, and I think you'll like what you see. Lorraine's company have surpassed themselves with the genetic modified bacteria, and we're ready to start production.'

'You're too generous,' Lorraine laughed. 'But you guys carry on. I'm going to take a look at the production schedule; I'll catch up with you later. By the way, Robert, we only have an hour here, so be ready to leave promptly.' Lorraine smiled at them both and then started to walk away.

'Sure,' Jerry replied. 'I'll get your man back in time, don't you worry.' Lorraine stopped and looked back at Robert. They both smiled uncomfortably, a little embarrassed at the notion that Robert was "her man".

'I don't know how much Lorraine has told you about the process, Robert,' Jerry said. 'But this bacteria that Lorraine's company provides generates two enzymes that sequentially break down PET Plastic into terephthalic acid and ethylene glycol. These are the two raw materials from which plastics such as PET are manufactured. At low levels, neither is harmful in the environment. However, this bacterium can further digest both substances to provide themselves with energy. First, we have to collect the plastic and chop it up into smaller pieces. Let's start over here,' Jerry said, leading Robert up a small incline towards what looked like a dam wall. There were hidden concrete steps, behind dense green foliage, next to a high wall. Jerry started up the steps, and Robert followed him.

At the top of the steps, the jungle broke open, and Robert squinted in the brightness of the full sun. After the darkness of the dense, dark forest, he needed a moment to adjust.

The view was stunning; the top step finished on top of the dam wall, above the dense jungle in brilliant sunshine. To the left of him, the land fell away into a valley, and he could see glimpses of the coast in the distance; to his right, following the line of the dam wall, overhung with more dense jungle, appeared a white, glistening river. Robert looked at Jerry, confused. It seemed surreal, but he didn't know what he was looking at.

'Yes,' announced Jerry. 'It's plastic.'

The strange 'ribbon' of plastic stretched back through the jungle for at least a mile. As Robert's eyes adjusted, he was able to pick out a massive confusion of white lumps, bumps and occasional coloured lids and labels. The plastic river narrowed and disappeared as it turned into the trees in the distance.

'My God!' exclaimed Robert. 'What the hell is this?'

'It's just what you see,' said Jerry. 'A river of plastic, literally.'

'How did it get here?'

'Well, quite naturally, really.'

'What do you mean, "naturally"? How could it be natural?'

'Well, all this plastic was already here when we looked at this land for the digester. It's accumulated from the merger of three rivers into this one. All this refuse is washed into the rivers from the towns upstream. It has been collecting here for decades.'

'Look here.' Jerry beckoned to Robert to follow him on a short walk around the dam wall. The wall they walked on was two metres wide, damp and strewn with vegetation. 'Watch your step, the humidity and algae here have made it quite slippery.'

'The river used to continue down there,' Jerry said, pointing to the foot of the dam. 'We built this wall to hold back the plastic, and let the water runoff over here, so we can direct it into a shredder.'

As Robert continued around the curved dam path, a corrugated roof covering a small weir came into view. As they approached the spillway, it became clear that the plastic river was being funnelled into this channel. Although plastic entered the sluice at quite a rate, it had no impact on the large backed-up plastic supply along the river; that didn't move at all.

'You see, most of this rubbish is air, empty bottles, bags, containers, and there's probably a couple of thousand tonnes backed up here, although it looks a lot more. We shred the plastic into one-centimetre chips that are fed into the digesters. There is a mechanism here, it has rotary gears with spurs that grab plastic from the river as it flows in and moves the pieces deeper into the shredder to get chopped up. We've found that one-centimetre chips are the most efficient size for the digesters.'

'Digesters? What are they?' asked Robert, amazed with what he saw.

'You'll see. Come this way.'

Robert followed Jerry as he descended another set of concrete steps. They passed by the shredder, which was pumping and clacking away rhythmically, and they headed to the other side of the main building.

The ground was wet and was particularly muddy at the bottom of the steps. Large mounds of red soil jutted up irregularly across the whole area.

Jerry walked up to a large, single-storey building that resembled an old rusty shipping container. 'This is one of our digesters.' He slapped the side of the building, and a hollow metallic clang echoed out. He laughed. 'This is where all the magic happens, in Big Bertha!'

The digester was at least three metres tall and twelve metres long. Above the digester, at one end, was a hopper that fed in the plastic pellets from the shredders.

Although he had initially mistaken the building for a rusty metal shipping container, Robert now saw that it had rounded ends, formed from newly welded, shiny metal plates, making it look torpedo shaped. Two pipes entered near the base, about one metre off of the ground, and larger pipes entered near the roof of the tank. At the far end, there was an access door, secured by a wheeled gear that gave it the look of a landlocked submarine.

Above the digester, a control room was positioned on a gantry-type arrangement, with pipes and cables linking the gantry and control room to the tank. A dim light shone from the window of the office. Robert could see Lorraine up there.

Jerry explained. 'We built three digesters, designed to take the Xylene and Tetrahydride acid by-products from PET digestion off to feed into those tall tanks, to use to synthesise new plastic.' Jerry pointed to two taller tanks.

'However, halfway through installation here Lorraine's team modified the bacteria significantly, to further digest those by-products into water and CO_2. We were quite happy with that, as the Xylene by-product is a solvent that can be quite toxic and flammable, so we had chemical engineers design a good safe extraction route via pipes. Some are still here,' Jerry said pointing to some pipes jutting out of the digester, and others partially disconnected from the gantry running to the tall tanks. 'They also generated a lot of heat. So, we needed to add several heat exchangers over there.' He pointed to two smaller, square silver units slightly behind the digester. 'The new process is safer, and we can recover heat from the process and provide the energy for all the processes on site, independent of any additional power.' Jerry smiled, proud of their self-sufficiency.

'So, you haven't got the final bacterial version yet?' asked Robert

'No, Lorraine's team are modifying the genome of the bacteria, to make it more efficient, quicker to digest plastic, with fewer by-products,' Jerry replied.

Jerry turned the wheel on the door, opening it wide. Robert peered in. It smelt sweet, humid and quite warm. He saw some little indicator lights flashing on a cluster of probes at the ceiling of the digester.

'As this bacteria need oxygen to grow, throughout the operation, we pump in compressed air and regulate the temperature and acidity of the process. Those probes monitor water, PH and oxygen levels.' Jerry pointed to the top of the digester. 'This controls everything, so it operates optimally, maximises digestion and reduces any remaining plastic or by-products.

'Robert, note that we keep this door shut at all times; it stops wildlife and other contaminants getting in.' Robert observed that a "No Entry" sign was stuck on the door, and there was a "Keep Closed" sign above the door on the wall of the tank.

Robert was amazed; it really seemed like he was witnessing the beginning of the end of all plastic waste in the world. 'What are the by-products?' he asked.

'Well, none really, the process takes ten days, and each digester takes twenty tonnes of plastic chips. At the end of the process, the bacteria die and sink to the bottom of the tank, just like in beer brewing, when the yeast runs out of sugar and nutrients and sinks to the bottom of the vat. But in this process, we recover heat throughout the process, and then at the end of the process, sterilise the tank with the reclaimed heat and then cool the dead bacteria and water. We can then safely pump it out, and the dry waste can be ploughed into fields or bagged as a fertiliser. We then start again with a new twenty-tonne batch of plastics in the digester.'

'Incredible. So...' Robert started slowly, 'to try and summarise, the plastic pellets enter here, and are mixed with water, and agitated, and then you add some bacteria that digest twenty tonnes of plastic in ten days and produce no by-products except water, CO_2 and fertiliser?'

'Yes, although for the first four days the bacteria are doubling, so most digestion occurs in the last six days.' Jerry laughed.

'Amazing. What's the catch?' asked Robert. 'Why doesn't every town have one? Why aren't these selling like hotcakes?'

'Robert, you must remember this is blue sky technology. This is a prototype that has been running for several months now, with several different types of genetically modified bacteria. Each new type has been significantly better than the previous one. We've tweaked the digester design to benefit from the bacterial enhancements. We are almost at a steady design to expand across to other sites.'

'And this bacteria have come from GM Agro-Tech? Lorraine's company?'

'Yes, that's correct.'

'Who has funded all this?' Robert asked.

'Well, this has been funded by a consortium of petrochemical companies, but run by Butler Oil & Gas. The consortiums were formed several years ago to bring funds together to focus on reducing the amount of plastic waste, which many people feel that the petrochemical industry has caused.'

'Probably a guilt thing,' he added. 'After all, directors in these companies have kids as well.' He smiled.

'But honestly,' pushed Robert, 'what is the downside? What are the risks? Are health and safety an issue? Toxicity, power consumption?'

'No, Robert. Sorry. The only downside I can see, is what if this digestion wasn't contained?'

'What do you mean?' asked Robert.

'Well, you can see what happens to plastic within these digesters; what if this bacteria could grow outside of these warm digesters? What effect would it have on the other plastic in the world, like non-rubbish, useful plastic?'

#

After leaving Jerry and Robert, Lorraine had headed off to the gantry to check on the digester settings and trial run profiles. She was interested to see how this latest bacteria performed against the last version. All her testing had been done on small-scale bioreactors and scale up was always a little hit and miss. Sometimes the strains performed better at a much larger scale, other times not so. She had always experienced a time delay in getting data back from the production facilities. Although the Memorandum of Understanding was supposed to provide more trust and allow easier data transfer between the organisations.

In the gantry, Lorraine saw several technicians carrying clipboards and keying information into the computers. She approached one technician, who turned to look at her. Lorraine flashed her ID and smiled. 'Excuse me, is there somewhere I can get this sample analysed, please?'

'Hi, Miss Bell-a-my.' The technician read her name slowly from her ID card. 'Sure, lady, head down those stairs to the microbiology assay room. Come I'll show you.' Lorraine thanked the man and followed him down the stairs to the now clearly sign-posted assay lab. 'What do you want to run?' he asked. 'Gene analysis or effluent toxicity?' Lorraine paused and stared at him, unsure of what she wanted.

'Sorry, I should explain; these are our standard tests: gene analysis to characterise the bacteria during production, and the effluent toxicity test to be sure that there are no toxic chemicals before we pump the waste out.'

'Could we do both?' she asked.

'Sure,' he answered. 'Getting your money's worth, I see.' He smiled.

'How long will it take?' she asked.

'About five minutes for this one,' he replied, as he pushed open large double doors into the assay laboratory.

'This gene sequencer is amazing,' he said, patting the analyser. 'And gas chromatography on this takes about 30 seconds.'

Lorraine thanked him and gave him the sample. She watched him load the sample, pressed a few buttons, and the process began.

After a brief pause, the technician exclaimed; 'I don't know where you got this from, lady, but the acid levels are off the scale. They are very concentrated. I've diluted it twice, and it's still off the scale. Hmm, apparently it's tetrahydric acid at almost a molar concentration.'

'That's impossible!' Lorraine was equally shocked. 'This is a sample of seawater.'

'Well it's not like any sea water I've ever analysed,' he replied. 'You've also got a quite high concentration of Xylene in this, but not as much as the acid.'

There was an intermittent beeping, and he turned to the gene analyser. 'Ah, okay, this one's ready now. Hmm, that's quite a quick identity check. It must be something that we have in our database already.'

'What is it? What do you mean?' Lorraine asked.

He looked, if anything, even more, surprised. 'Well, it's an E Coli, a gene-modified E Coli, but...' He looked at a datasheet next to the sequencer machine. 'Yes, it's definitely one we've had here before. Where did you say you got this, lady?' He pressed a few more buttons on the gene sequencer. It started whirring again.

'It's from a seawater sample,' Lorraine replied. 'Why?'

'It really looks like one we tested, a GM bacteria we tried here about six months ago and gave up on. It was far too aggressive. It dissolved plastic quickly, but it also damaged our metal probes and pitted metal containers.'

'Really?' Lorraine said, interested. 'You said it was a genetically modified bacteria. Do you know what strain it was?'

The gene sequencer beeped, and some printed ticker tape came out of the machine.

'Yes,' he replied, looking at the results. 'We have it labelled as IS-23.'

Chapter 12

Lorraine headed down the gantry steps to find Robert talking with Jerry at the heat exchangers near the digester.

'Robert, we have just enough time to get back to the hotel to pick up our bags and get to the airport. I'm afraid that's the end of the tour.'

'No problem, Lorraine,' Robert said.

'Jerry that was fantastic I hope we can talk again. It's an incredible facility.' Robert was buzzing from what he had seen and learned.

'Guys, you are more than welcome. I hope to see you both again soon.'

Robert turned to Lorraine and took her hand. 'Thanks for bringing me and organising this tour. It was fantastic.'

Lorraine smiled nervously and pulled her hand away. She now had evidence that GM Agro-Tech was involved in the tragedy that had afflicted the fishermen, and the strange incident that Jane had been involved in. The sample results were quite clear: the water was contaminated with the IS-23 genetically modified bacteria. This was a profoundly worrying issue. Should she contact Hugh, and find out what happened? Should she confide in Robert? But then he wouldn't be happy that her company were somehow involved in his daughter's accident.

She decided that now was not the time to discuss it; she trailed behind Robert, feeling confused, as they walked towards the car.

#

The scenery that Robert and Lorraine saw below them on Bioko Island, the home to Malobo, the capital of Equatorial Guinea, was breath-taking. The valleys, the high, mountainous jungle, and the steppe, reminded Robert of scenes from Jurassic Park. A vast lake in a dormant volcano dominated the centre of the island.

As the plane banked and began its descent, Robert murmured 'It's strange...'

'What is?' asked Lorraine.

'That this is such a beautiful island, and yet its people are so poor.'

'Why is that strange?' she asked. 'Many countries are poor.'

'But Equatorial Guinea is one of the richest countries in Africa. It has a Gross Domestic Product per capita of $38,000, it brings in over 9 billion dollars of oil revenue each year, and its people are still some of the poorest in the world.'

'Are you sure? The roads and facilities look fairly good.'

'Well yes, the president has invested a lot in infrastructure, but that's mainly to retain foreign investment in oil exploration and refinery, not for his people. Look,' Robert said, pointing out of the window. 'Bioko's Liquid Petroleum Gas Refinery, one of the biggest in the world.' From their airborne vantage point, the northeast of the island came into view, and some substantial white storage silos were now visible. A massive expanse of concrete infrastructure surrounded the silos. The plane banked again, and view through the window changed back to green mountains. The landing gear descended, and the aircraft touched the runway.

#

Robert and Lorraine negotiated their way through airport security, dodged a few hawkers in the airport entrance, and flagged down a taxi into the city centre.

They got out of the taxi at the address they had been given, next to a Café Noir on the Av. del 3 de Agosto in Malabo. Lorraine looked around, confused and asked, 'Robert, are you sure about this?'

'What was Freddie thinking?' Robert thought as he and Lorraine stood on the pavement and looked in vain for a bookshop.

Several of these blocks had shops at road level. They looked up and down the road until Lorraine noticed a small "book store" sign above a grocery store.

The bookshop that Freddie had booked for the signing turned out to be a grocery store on a road of fairly nondescript five-storey apartment buildings.

As Robert and Lorraine entered the grocery shop, they saw a corner at the back of the store dedicated to second-hand books. There was a single chair next to a round table that had been set with a teapot next to a cup and saucer. To reaffirm to the two incredulous visitors that this was indeed intended for Robert, someone had put a copy of his book on the table. 'Oh, Robert how charming, look they knew you were English,' Lorraine laughed, pointing at the teapot and cup.

'Yes,' Robert replied grumpily. 'Hardly tea at the Ritz, though, is it?'

'Oh cheer up, Robert. There are no press hounds here! It should be an easy ride.'

A small lady emerged from behind the till and held her arms out in greeting. Senor Howdon, how very nice to meet you,' she said in English with a heavy Spanish accent.

'Welcome to the Malabo Book Store,' she added, smiling.

Robert glanced at Lorraine. 'Note that she said "the" Book Store! There are no others in the capital, then.' He whispered and grimaced and then smiled back at the lady. Lorraine giggled, and Robert found himself doing the same.

The lady ushered them into the corner. Robert sat down, and took his pen out of his pocket, ready to sign books. Since there was only a single chair, Lorraine stood next to the table beside Robert. Freddie had told him he would have two hours to sign books and mingle! Apart from the occasional shopper who wandered in and looked at him as they took products off the shelves, there was very little in the way of mingling. At one moment a lady approached, and he thought he might actually sign a book, but he was dismayed to be asked to hand a book down from a high shelf. He obliged but rolled his eyes in disappointment when he saw it was a Barbara Cartland novel. Lorraine laughed loudly and got a dirty look from the lady for her troubles.

An hour into the ordeal, Robert had more or less lost the will to live. 'Right, I think it's time to go. This has been a total waste of time. I've neither signed my name nor mingled with people, and the only book that's changed hands was by Barbara bloody Cartland.'

Robert put his pen back in his pocket and got ready to leave. Just as a wizened old lady entered the shop. He turned to Lorraine, prepared to usher her out of the store when he realised that the old lady was approaching him.

'Senor Robert?' she enquired, in a tremulous voice, husky with age and too many cigarettes.

'Yes, Robert Howdon,' he replied and held his hand out to greet the old lady.

'Oh, Senor Robert.' She bowed and kissed his hand and started to weep. Robert was quite taken aback and looked at Lorraine. She was as surprised as he was, but recovered her composure to help the old lady to her feet.

'Oh, I'm sorry, so sorry for your daughter's accident, you poor man. I pray for her. Poor girl,' she said, still clasping Robert's hand, now on her feet and looking directly into his eyes.

'She is much better,' Robert replied. 'Thank you so much, but please don't be concerned, she...'

'I saw her, I saw what she looked like, and the poor boy with her. Terrible,' she went on. 'You take care of her like I take care of my brother.'

'Your brother?' Lorraine asked gently.

'Yes,' the old lady replied. 'My brother also had the same problems, his face was blistered, and his eyes were swollen, terrible.'

'What happened to him?' asked Lorraine.

'The same thing,' the lady said. 'Fishing in that sea.' She spat on the ground and crossed herself. 'Many poor men died out there, but Bartho survived. Thank god.' She crossed herself again.

Lorraine and Robert looked at each other. 'Was he the fisherman that survived the storm?' Robert asked.

'Storm? There was no storm.' She held up her fingers as though grasping an imaginary grape. 'Storm does not do that, authorities lie, no storm. Quiet work, very hush-hush. But Bartho knows, he knows what happened and no one listens.'

'I'd be very interested in listening,' said Robert. 'Can we meet him?'

'Si, I can take you, we do not live far away. This is very kind Senor Robert, you are a good man.' She bent to kiss his hand again and patted his arm.

Robert told the lady at the cash till he was going, apologising for leaving early, but he signed his only book and handed to her. She nodded, smiling, and thanked him. Both ladies chatted and gestured to each other and then Robert and Lorraine followed the old lady out of the shop.

#

The old lady walked slowly and steadily for two blocks, turned into a two-storey apartment block and opened a door on the ground floor.

They followed her in. The apartment, although immaculately clean, looked dated, and had a medical, almost hospital smell. 'Please sit,' she instructed, pointing to the settee, which was decorated with crocheted lace head rests and arm protectors and wandered off to another room.

They heard a muffled conversation between two voices, and then she returned to the room. 'He'll be along soon,' she said. 'You want to drink something?' she asked.

'Yes please,' replied Lorraine, 'if it isn't too much trouble.'

'Not at all,' the lady replied and left the room.

The door opened and a man older in appearance than his years shuffled out. 'Hello, hello,' he said hoarsely, smiling and obviously pleased to have guests. 'Aleta told me she was going to meet you. I'm sorry about your daughter, Robert. I hope she is recovering well.' He walked forward to shake Robert's hand and, as he emerged from the shadows, his features became visible. Lorraine took an intake of breath as Bartho's face came into the light. He wore a patch over one eye and his face looked bloated and scarred. His skin was red, and he had several open, ulcerated sores. She could see the remnants of some cream that had been spread about his neck and his hair was matted and stuck partially to his head.

'Apologies for my appearance, but believe me, this is a vast improvement since three months ago.' Bartho's voice was rough, but he spoke English well.

Aleta spoke in Spanish to him and gesticulated. 'My sister thinks you are interested in my story. We saw your daughter and her friends on TV, and it seemed more than coincidence that she and her friends should have similar injuries to mine and be seen in the same harbour.' Aleta murmured something else to him.

'Si, yes, the boat they had in tow was like the one I used.'

'We are very interested in your story. What happened to you, Bartho, will you tell us?' Robert replied.

Bartho shuffled over to a nearby armchair and sat down. He called his sister over and clasped her hands. I'm sorry Aleta I've hidden some of this truth from you.'

She patted his hand and said, 'Okay Bartho, don't worry my dear. Go ahead.'

Bartho explained how he and fifteen other men who congregated at the harbour each day for casual labour were paid to travel to a plastic gyre which had collected over the years. It was about five miles off the coast. Each week, for several months, they sprayed a liquid on the surface and measured the depth of the plastic island. They travelled at night, in fishing gear, so as not to arouse suspicion. Over the weeks the smell got stronger, the land started to move more, and there was death in the air. It stank of dead fish, and the carcasses of animals and birds had begun to litter the island.

On the last visit, he and the other men were overcome by fumes, which blistered his skin and lungs and later caused an infection that led him to lose his eye, as antibiotics couldn't control his skin infection. All the other men died, but he managed to survive. He was devastated that so many of the men he had got to know had died, but at the same time, realised that he was fortunate to survive. He finished by making a crucifix on his chest and wiping away a tear from his remaining eye. He was also lucky that Aleta had come looking for him, other men that had migrated from the centre of the country had no family to look for them or bury them. 'Aleta was here for me,' he said holding Aleta's hand. 'I'm very lucky.'

'Thank you for telling us this you poor man,' Lorraine said with a tear in her eye. 'But why didn't you go to the police?'

'I wanted to,' Bartho replied. 'But the harbour master told the press a story about a storm, and I had no papers, everyone else was dead. Who would have believed my story?'

Robert suddenly realised how close Jane had come to getting seriously injured. 'Bartho, thank you for sharing this with us. You have been through a terrible ordeal. I'm so very sorry for your loss.' Glancing at Lorraine, he added, 'Bartho, do you know how this happened?'

'I'm not sure,' Bartho said. 'The liquid we were spraying wasn't harmful, but over the months, the plastic island became less stable, it got thinner, like it was breaking up, or melting.'

Robert glanced at Lorraine. 'Like something was digesting the plastic?' Robert asked.

'Well, yes, I suppose so,' said Bartho.

'Do you remember if there was any writing on the equipment you were given, or who paid you?'

'Apart from several small flat-bottomed boats, we had very little equipment, and we were paid cash by a man at the harbour. Just the measuring rods, and the spray tanks, and pads to write down the figures. Sorry, that's all I know.'

'You don't need to apologise, Bartho, you've been through a lot, and you've been very helpful,' said Robert. 'But if you can think of anything else, please call me.' Robert handed over a piece of paper with his details on it.

'I am sorry, though, sorry I can't help you more. Since my illness, I can only recall fragments of what happened out there.' Bartho stopped, looking into the far distance as if something had come to his mind. 'I do remember seeing a number 23 somewhere, and the man who paid us was called Senor Adam.'

Lorraine went pale and audibly gulped. Robert glanced at her. 'Are you okay, Lorraine?'

'Yes. Thanks. It…It's just I'm aware that an early bacterial strain was called IE-23, and it was able to digest plastic at a rapid rate. Could this all be connected?'

'Bartho,' Lorraine asked, 'on the boats windscreen, do you remember any pictures at all? Near the harbour ID disc?'

'Yes, sort of. I remember a kind of cartoon, something yellow, like a banana, no, more like a corn husk.'

Lorraine and Robert looked at each other.

Chapter 13

Robert and Lorraine thanked Bartho and Aleta for their time, they walked back to the main road near the bookstore and hailed a taxi heading back to the airport for the flight back to Port Bata.

Robert broke the uncomfortable silence between them.

'I've been a fool,' he said. 'A bloody fool.'

Lorraine looked at him quizzically. 'Why do you say that?' she asked.

'Because I was so keen to speak with you, to discuss my work, and the science, with someone, I forgot to be wary. I trusted you, and you've known all along.'

'Why wary? And what have I known all along, Robert? This is all news to me, as it is for you.'

'Why are you here, exactly?' Robert asked 'How come you know about the bacterial work here that nearly killed my daughter and Bartho. You saw Bartho. What sort of work is your company doing?'

Lorraine suddenly felt out of her depth: the science, the funding, the excitement of travelling and meeting Robert. It now felt so uncomfortable and overwhelming she didn't know what to say.

Should she tell Robert everything she knew? The reason she was there? She feared losing her credibility with Robert and their friendship. She had accepted that their relationship could be no more than that; but if Robert didn't trust her anymore, losing a rare and exciting friendship would be hard to take.

She looked out of the taxi window, tears welling in her eyes. 'Robert, you must believe me, I knew nothing of this. About Bartho, about what was going on here, or the danger.' Her tears flowed freely now. 'You must believe me.'

'And why did you come here? Why to my hotel, the night after we arrived? This is all too coincidental.'

119

'Okay, Robert, I'll tell you. But please don't judge me; I only had the best intentions. I wanted to help you.'

Lorraine explained what Hugh had proposed, that night he had phoned her in London. He knew she had already met Robert, and thought the publicity would be good for Robert and GM Agro-Tech. She told Robert how Hugh had ordered her to come to Equatorial Guinea, and the strange request he had made, about keeping Robert out of the hospital. Only now had she realised that there was a connection between the accident that had injured Jane and GM Agro-Tech. Hugh obviously didn't want Robert establishing that link, much less Lorraine.

She also was aware that Hugh was trying to hide something.

She explained to Robert that she had read the dispatch authorisations at her laboratory before she left and saw that some older strains that should not have left their research facility had been sent to Equatorial Guinea, but not to the production facility. She suspected that these strains were the ones that had caused terrible injuries to Bartho and killed his colleagues. This strain was IS-23.

'So, you're telling me your company produced some killer bacteria, released it into the sea, and this killed the fishermen, nearly killed Bartho, and could have killed my daughter? And you knew none of this?'

'Robert, I knew about the strains we were developing and of the one that we were sending to the production facility, but I had no idea about any other activity out here,' she sobbed. 'Please believe me.'

Robert looked at Lorraine. He wanted to believe her, and he valued her friendship and their bond, but was she telling him the truth?

As he looked out the window, deep in thought, his mobile rang.

'Hello,' he answered.

'Daddy, it's Jane.'

'Hello, darling, what's up? Are you okay?'

'Yes. Juan asked me if you were around to visit the old village. He said you had planned to go there sometime.'

'Yes, Juan did mention this in the hospital, we're still on our way back from Malabo. I think it will be too late to go by the time we get back, but what about tomorrow?'

'Okay, hang on.' Jane turned to Juan, who was sitting next to her in the campus restaurant and said, 'Dad's interested, but he's travelling right now; could you go tomorrow?'

Juan nodded. 'Yes, tomorrow is also good.'

'Daddy, Juan thinks tomorrow is fine,' Jane said, turning back to her mobile phone.

'Ok, tell Juan I'll meet him at the campus tomorrow morning, at about ten, if that's ok.'

Juan nodded, and Jane said, 'Yes, that's good for Juan too, Daddy.'

'Thanks, Jane, sounds like we have a plan. Take care now. Bye.'

Robert hung up and again turned to the window, collecting his troubled thoughts.

'We need to get to the bottom of this, Lorraine.' He spoke softly. 'Juan is taking us to a village tomorrow, which he thinks looked and smelt like the plastic island they hit in the boat. It might shed more light on this whole thing. I think I need you to be there, and I want to trust you.'

'Thank you, Robert. Of course, I'll come. You have to trust me. I've told you everything.'

'But tell me, Lorraine, how did you know Jane was in the hospital?'

He watched Lorraine go through some kind of internal struggle, then she said, 'Hugh told me you were visiting her, and what hotel you were in, but I had no idea of why, or what she was doing here.'

'So how did Hugh know this?' Robert mused. Lorraine shook her head. 'I really have no idea.'

Robert still wasn't sure that he trusted Lorraine completely, but he could see she was doing her best, to be honest with him. Whether that would be enough, he didn't know.

As the taxi made its leisurely way to the airport, Robert mulled over what Bartho had said about the incident. Robert Googled the news around the date of the event. Searching for the keywords "fishermen", "deaths" and "storm". He read that local authorities had attributed the incident to stormy seas in the area. They speculated that a fuel leak on a boat had caused the skin lesions on the dead men and the sole survivor, whom he now knew to be Bartho. Robert looked further down the report, to the comments section, and saw that some people were demanding an investigation. But most of the fishermen were of unknown origin or addresses, likely migrants from the centre of the region, looking for casual work. There were suggestions that the men's work was involved with spraying chemicals on a gyre. Robert guessed these may have been comments raised by several relatives of the men who presumably felt they were being fobbed off and wanted more answers.

Under one of the comments making demands for answers, he saw one that made a causal link between the boats registered with GM Agro-Tech and the work carried out on the gyres. Robert 'liked' that posting and added a comment: 'Do you think GM Agro-Tech was the cause of these men's deaths, and can we discuss evidence? Contact Robert Howdon at #RHowdon,' and he submitted his post.

#

The taxi drew up at their hotel. It was a little after nine in the evening and the night air was warm and dry. Robert paid the taxi driver, thanking him, and walked into the foyer with Lorraine.

'Robert I'm sorry, but I feel exhausted. I think I'll go up to my room straight away.' Lorraine yawned.

Robert agreed. 'Yes, I'm feeling drained too, I think I'll turn in.'

They exchanged a brief hug and said good night, and made their way to their respective rooms. Robert headed up the stairs, and Lorraine made her way to her ground floor room behind reception.

#

Across a chain of corporate web servers, digital robots – bots – sifted through millions of social network postings. They stirred into action when any digital content; whether a posting, news article or email, containing the term "GM Agro Tech" was encountered. Automatic reports were generated recording the words used, the context, the location and the originator.

Two people, in particular, were made aware by mobile alerts of the new internet material intercepted from social media postings, containing the keywords "GM Agro-Tech", "Deaths", "evidence" and the location "Equatorial Guinea".

And the source: '#RHowdon.'

Chapter 14

The next morning, Lorraine woke to sunlight shining in through the French doors of her ground floor veranda. She opened the doors and looked out onto the hotel gardens. She closed her eyes and smelt the warm aromatic air. The curtains billowed with the gentle breeze, and cicadas chirped outside rhythmically She turned towards the bathroom to run a shower.

Lorraine undressed in the bathroom, slipped on a hotel bathrobe and tied up her hair, then picked up yesterday's clothes and placed them in a plastic laundry bag next to her case. She paused, with her head up, sensing her surroundings. Something was different. What was it? The breeze had subsided, but there was something else. She realised that the crickets had fallen silent, had something disturbed them, she wondered. Lorraine then turned to look outside when a figure stepped into the light shining in through the French doors, blocking the sunlight and casting a dark shadow into the room.

She felt her breath catch in her throat, a bubble of fear, and then she recognised Hugh. 'Hugh, you made me jump! What do you want? It's very early.'

'I just thought I'd pop by. Check how things are with you and Robert.' His voice was oddly flat and emotionless. 'What have you been up to?' Before Lorraine could speak, he added, 'But I should say thanks for getting Robert away from the hospital.' He gave a brief smile. 'Things are better now. There was a little mess we needed to clear up, but it's all in hand now.'

'Well, Hugh, I'm sorry, but I don't think so,' Lorraine replied. 'We saw Bartho yesterday, the only survivor from the group of fishermen who died here. He knows that you sprayed the gyre with bacteria from strain IS-23, and he knows the cause of their deaths wasn't a storm, as the press seem to believe. Hugh, what have you done?'

Hugh rolled his eyes. 'What the hell have you been doing? What has this got to do with a book signing? Why didn't you just keep out of this?'

'Hugh, don't you realise that Robert's daughter could have been killed? That's why Bartho wanted to talk to us. He told us what had happened to him. The same thing happened to Jane and her friends, didn't it? They were injured in the same way as Bartho and his companions. They were just a bit luckier, and got away with their lives.'

'Lorraine, have you seen the comments Robert made about GM Agro-Tech on Twitter? Do you know how much damage he is doing? He will lose us our jobs and shut down GM Agro-Tech if this continues.'

'I don't know what you mean, Hugh, Robert has been with me all day.'

'Of course, he has, but he has also been making comments on Twitter, comments that are libellous and damaging to us.'

'Robert wouldn't do that unless he had a good reason,' Lorraine answered.

'For god's sake, Lorraine, think about it! He has indicted the company, and you and me along with it. You should have done something to stop this happening. I wanted you to get us some positive publicity, not a whole bunch of litigious comments that could seriously harm us.'

'The thing is, Hugh, Robert is probably right. There are a lot of things that don't add up. I don't know if it's you or the company that has caused this, and I certainly don't know what the plan is here, but whatever it is people are getting hurt, and it has to stop.'

Hugh's fury was etched on his face. 'You dare to tell me what to start or stop? You have no fucking idea what's going on here.' Hugh's voice rose to a shout as his anger boiled over.

'Perhaps if you told us what's going on, we'd be able to help,' Lorraine said, in an attempt to defuse the situation. But Hugh was far too furious to listen to anything she said.

'Help? Help? Are you fucking joking, Lorraine? You'd just go and cause more trouble.' Hugh grabbed Lorraine by the throat. 'You listen to me. You'd better fucking sort it out with Robert, give him some spin, something to get those posts removed, or I swear I'm going to kill you!' He released his grip and Lorraine fell forward.

'You wouldn't dare,' she gasped, standing upright again, holding her neck. 'I know you're implicated in all this. You signed for those bacteria shipments, you had them brought here, and you're obviously part of whatever caused these accidents. And I know you've been keeping an eye on Jane. You were recognised at the hospital, for god's sake.'

Hugh's eyes widened. He grabbed her neck again and tightened his grip. She winced and struggled for breath. He slammed her onto the bed. 'I'm warning you. No more games.' He smiled grimly, and with his other hand pointed a mock gun at her head with his finger and mimicked firing it. She gasped for air and started hitting his arm and kicking to break his grip.

There was a knock at the door. Hugh looked at the door and back to Lorraine.

'You've been warned,' he said. With a quick glance at the door, walked briskly out through the open French doors, into the garden, and disappeared.

Lorraine was shaken to the core. She was panting, taking deep breaths to recover. Had Hugh just tried to kill her? She went to the bathroom, shaking, held onto the sink and stared into the mirror hanging over it, then took a deep breath. Trying to suppress the tears she could feel stinging her eyes. There was a knock at the door again. 'Lorraine, are you there?' It was Robert's voice.

'Won't be a minute,' she called out. She then ran the taps and splashed some cold water on her face and hair. She gathered her bathrobe around herself, pulling the collar up to hide her red neck and grabbed a towel.

'I'm coming,' she said, walking to the door, pretending to dry her hair.

She opened the door for Robert. 'I'm sorry, I was in the shower. I didn't hear you.'

'No problem, it's just we are running late, I wanted to check you were okay.'

'Yes, I'm fine.'

'Are you sure?' he asked. 'You look a little pale.'

'Just let me put some lipstick on, and I'll be fine.' She did her best to smile.

'Okay,' he laughed. 'I'll see you downstairs, then.'

The breakfast room in the hotel was quite empty; maybe it had more tourists staying than working folk.

'Lorraine, I've invited Jerry to come with us today, I thought with what he knows about the production and stuff he might find this trip interesting.'

'Jerry? Yes, sure. Good idea.'

She seemed a little distracted. Robert wondered if she was going off the idea, or wasn't feeling well.

'Are you okay to go?' he asked.

'Yes, of course,' she smiled. But it wasn't her full smile.

'Good morning,' Jerry said, cheerfully, as he walked into the breakfast area. 'May I?' he asked just a second after he had picked up a piece of Robert's toast.

'Want some coffee?' asked Lorraine, picking a new cup from another table and pouring one for him.

'Thanks.' He smiled happily at Lorraine through a mouthful of toast. 'By the way I've got my Discovery outside, I thought your car might be a little tight for the four of us.

They set off for the campus, where they met Juan waiting at the entrance. Everyone noticed how much better he was looking. The swelling around his face had gone down, although it was still slightly red. He was smiling broadly and greeted them warmly. 'Hello, sirs, and Miss Lorraine.'

They all greeted him as he got into the car.

'How was your trip to Malabo?' asked Juan.

'It was fascinating,' said Robert. 'Apart from the book signing.'

'Why was that?' asked Jerry.

'I didn't get to sign any books,' he laughed.

'Miss Lorraine, I tested my samples,' said Juan.

'Oh yes?' she said. 'What did you find?'

'Well, not a lot,' Juan replied. 'They were very acidic, and there was some bacterial growth, but I couldn't tell what.'

'I also looked at the sample, Juan, and you are correct; it was a strain of E Coli. It appears that the bacteria was generating high levels of acid and xylene by-products.'

'One thing I found interesting; I measured the turbidity of the samples,' Juan added.

'That's good thinking,' said Jerry. 'We've thought about adding that test within our digesters, but we haven't got around to it yet. What did you find?'

'Well, the turbidity of the water was really high. The thickening of the water was due to the number of micro-plastic particles that were present in the seawater in the area. I've never seen anything like it. It certainly wasn't any algae bloom.

'I can see that measuring the turbidity of the digesters would help ensure that no micro-plastics are discarded. Perhaps if there were any remaining, we could sieve them out to ensure none were introduced back to the sea or the land. We could re-introduce them to the next digestion batch.' Jerry was enjoying the discussion. He looked over his shoulder at Juan, and Robert winced, expecting the car to veer off the rough road at any moment.

'I didn't realise there was so much plastic in the sea,' said Lorraine. 'Surely that's not everywhere. I've never seen any plastic along beaches.'

'Ah, Miss Lorraine, plastic waste is collecting in the oceans into huge islands around the world. There are five particularly big ones, called gyres. The wind and tides push them together. The biggest one is estimated to cover six hundred thousand square miles and is in the middle of the Pacific. But there are also smaller, breakaway ones. There is one off the coast here which I think we sailed close to the other day.'

'Juan, I think you're the only one of us to have seen one first-hand,' said Robert.

Juan shrugged. 'No I don't it was. It was more than that. It was more chemical pollution I think. Although there was some plastic, there wasn't a proper plastic gyre. The water was red, and I really don't know what was in there, or where the acid or micro-plastics came from.'

Robert stated the obvious; obvious to all but Juan. 'Well, it seems to me that someone has been spraying bacteria onto a plastic gyre to dissolve the plastic. But in the process of doing that, they have made the water toxic with acid and xylene and generated micro-plastics that are making the water turbid.'

'Is that possible?' asked Juan. 'Who would do that? The micro-plastics would kill the marine life; although it's true we did see many dead animals in that red water.'

Lorraine and Robert looked at each other.

Robert was aware that Lorraine didn't want to suggest the link with her organisations, and Jerry was also unaware of the connection. *Now's not the time to make everyone aware,* thought Robert.

'I think I can see another use for a digester,' mused Jerry. 'If we had a digester on container ships, they could scoop up bits of a gyre at each pass and digest them. They could even sieve up micro-plastics, like filter feeding whales do, to take them out of the water.'

'That's a great idea,' Robert smiled. 'I think that could really work, especially if one of those ocean pontoons was used to ring-fence them first.'

The drive continued along the coast road north for about five kilometres, and then curved inland, following alongside a dry riverbed.

Where the road crossed the river, they turned down an unmade track, through a dense part of the jungle that headed back towards the coast. As they continued down the narrow road, they passed wooden houses with corrugated metal roofs, open windows and doors left ajar. Approaching the centre of the village the buildings became more substantial and brick built, and some were quite ornate. There was what they guessed was a bank and another building that might possibly be a town hall. All were overgrown with vines and were in various stages of decay.

They stopped in the square and got out. A road ran down to a beach on their right; otherwise, they were entirely surrounded by abandoned buildings. Jungle seemed to fill in every gap.

'Welcome to Ngaba,' said Juan.

The village had obviously been deserted for some time. There was no sign of human habitation. There were rusting cars, and the odd wild dog ran between the buildings. Birds seemed comfortable with the visitors and didn't seem threatened.

'I brought the students here once several years ago. But I haven't been back,' said Juan.

Jerry had wandered into a building with the sign 'Comestibles'; probably once the village general store. It had no windows, and the door hung off its hinges. Any contents had long been ransacked. The air smelt acidic and sweet. The walls were stained with red streaks, and patches of red could be seen all around the store, at different heights, around the windows and the floor, the broken table and shelves of a broken freezer that lay with its door ajar.

'Look at this,' said Jerry. 'What is this? Algae? Mould?'

Juan came in after him. 'There is the same smell, and this is the same red colour; it's the same as we saw at sea.'

'But what is it?' asked Jerry. 'Mould would cover the whole wall, not just patches of it. Why would this cover shelves and occur in odd patches on the wall?'

Lorraine and Robert stepped in; they had been looking around in the adjacent buildings. 'Guys, do you know what is happening here?' Lorraine asked.

'No idea. I don't get it,' Jerry replied.

'Look,' Lorraine said. 'The red line is following the lines of plastic power conduit around the room, the plastic coating on the freezer shelves, and the plastic light switches and sockets.'

'No,' said Jerry. 'That would be too weird.' He scratched away some of the red pus-like growth with a piece of wood and found the metal components of a light switch. The square covering of the switch had been lost, dissolved into something unrecognisable. 'That's incredible,' he gasped.

They took a closer look around the village and found examples of misshapen guttering, partially dissolved linoleum, car dashboards and windscreen wipers melted out of shape, and plastic litter distorted into surreal shapes.

'This is terrible,' said Robert. 'Think about it. Plastic is ubiquitous in our lives. If we invent an organism able to dissolve one type of plastic, what's to stop it eating everything?'

'But we only want to dissolve waste plastic, pollution,' replied Juan.

'Yes, but how can you differentiate between pollution and the stuff you want to keep?' asked Jerry. 'Robert at the plant you asked me about a downside to the plastic digestion. This looks like this is it, although it doesn't look like the strains we use. We have no redness or strong smells like this!'

'Maybe there needs to be some governance over the types of plastic we produce,' suggested Lorraine. 'If we make bacteria that only dissolve a certain type of plastic, and we make bottles and single-use items out of that "sacrificial" plastic, and then we make the things that we need to keep, like light switches and computers, out of a plastic the bacteria can't dissolve. Would that work?'

'But what about when you throw them away?' asked Jerry. 'Then you do want them to be dissolved.'

'And if one country decides to make bacteria to digest another country's "governed" plastic, it could be used in warfare,' suggested Robert.

'Lorraine, what you have created needs protecting,' said Jerry. 'But I think we've possibly opened Pandora's Box, Pandora's plastic box!'

'But there is no suggestion that what happened here has anything to do with GM Agro-Tech, is there? Lorraine, is there?' asked Robert.

'I'll take some samples and run them through the lab. Find out for sure. But this does look suspiciously like what we've seen on the boats and from Juan's samples.'

'I've read that some wild bacteria have been found in landfill that can digest plastic, but I've not heard of anything at this scale in nature,' said Jerry. They looked at each other, trying to get their heads around the importance of what they saw, of the potential for disaster on a global scale. Juan woke them out of their worries and hustled them out of the old shop.

'This way, there is another place that I want to show you.'

He led them around one of the buildings towards a virtually dry riverbed that ran towards the shore further along the beach. 'No, we are not going down to the sea,' he said. 'Come with me.' He began to walk upstream. After only a short distance, the riverbed was packed with plastic waste.

They walked nearly fifty yards before they reached the end of the wall of plastic; the water level had increased, dramatically. It had been dammed by the plastics downstream. The water held back by the plastic dam was dark red and streaked with foam.

As they walked closer, the air became a toxic, pungent mix of a sweet and acidic smell; they coughed and gagged and felt burning sensations in their eyes and lungs.

'My God!' exclaimed Lorraine. 'The whole river is contaminated.' From their vantage point, they could see several miles upriver. The river continued, red, interspersed with white plastic debris and foam.

'Jerry, what temperature do you run your digesters at?' asked Robert.

'Between 26 and 30 degrees centigrade,' he replied.

'I'd suggest that the ambient temperature and humidity here near the equator is conducive to this bacteria living outside in the environment.'

'I'd agree,' said Jerry. 'If this is indeed bacteria of course.' 'How would we kill them or decontaminate? I know about sterilisation, but we can't attempt it on this scale. We have to find a way, though this can't be allowed to spread.' Robert said.

'We could use antibiotics,' said Lorraine, 'except if these are gram-negative bacteria, like E. coli of course. They are highly resistant to antibiotics.' Lorraine felt worried.

'Or phages,' suggested Juan.

'What are they?' asked Robert.

'There are specific species of virus that only target bacteria,' answered Lorraine.

'I think you have your next project lined up.' Jerry smiled bleakly at Lorraine. 'You have created a monster, and now you need to control it.'

'Jerry, if this is bacteria, we work for a company that profits from this technology, so we have a responsibility for it. But how did this process occur here? Naturally? Have these bacteria evolved here?'

'We can't rule out the possibility that GM Agro-Tech had a role here, can we?' said Robert. His face was grim.

'I guess we can't,' said Lorraine, startled by Robert's comment. Now she thought about it, she realised it was entirely possible. What had Hugh done? How far had he gone?

'But it's easy enough to find out. I'll take more samples,' she replied.

It was Jerry's turn to look grim. 'Juan, when did this happen to this town?'

'This has been deserted for at least 3 years.' Replied Juan.

'And what lies further up the river?' asked Robert.

'There is some light industry further upstream, some small manufacturing plants that are still going. But it's pretty much a dead end until you get to the Rio Mbini, near San Carlos.'

'That's the river that the production plant is on,' said Robert. 'Jerry, could this river have dried up when the production plant built the dam and diverted the river?'

'That's possible,' said Jerry. It's a similar timeframe, though I thought that the river we dammed followed the original source. But good call. It is possible that plastic waste has been washed down here, just as it has at the production facility. Maybe it came through another branch of the Rio Mbini.'

'Jerry, why would you plan to build your plant out here?' asked Robert.

'Well, as we can see, there is a lot of plastic waste here; though you could probably pick any African or Asian coastline and find the same thing at the end of any river. Plus, the emerging oil and gas industry here is bringing in big business, the tax incentives are favourable and dare I say it, the regulations around building, developing and testing solutions are fairly lax, certainly not up to the more stringent regulations of Europe or the US.'

'And where there's too much regulation, innovation is stifled,' said Lorraine.

'What do you mean by that?' asked Robert. 'I would have thought that your company would want regulation to protect your intellectual property?'

'You're probably right, I'm just repeating something someone once said to me. It just makes sense of why we strategically invested out here.'

'But you make a good point, Robert. Without regulation, you'd have no intellectual property to own and profit from, no investment, no standards to abide by,' said Jerry.

'And chaos can quickly set in without standards and regulations,' added Lorraine.

They turned to walk back to the car.

'Lorraine, I have some sample tubes here, shall we both take some?' asked Juan.

'Yes,' she agreed, and they each picked up four glass sample tubes from the car and took samples of the red extrusion from different areas of the town.

As she looked for another good place to take samples, Lorraine passed a child's dolls pram laying on its side. Lorraine stopped to stand the pram upright. Inside the pram, strapped within the seat was a child's doll, its face was deformed and partially digested. Lorraine felt physically sick.

Chapter 15

Jerry dropped Robert and Lorraine off back at the hotel. They said their good-byes to Jerry, and walked to the hotel terrace and sat at a small table with two chairs overlooking the gardens.

'Lorraine, I think we have enough evidence to bring a case against Hugh. And I also think we should alert the authorities about the gyre, and the deserted village at Ngaba. My concern is that your company may be implicated. What are your thoughts?'

'Oh, Robert, what a mess! I agree with you, but I would like to identify these samples, to be sure we are only talking about one strain.'

'Okay, so when we check the samples, do we inform your company? Call the police? We don't want the digesters closed down, but the situation needs to be assessed.'

'I think we need to check the samples before we decide what to do. But first, let's see if there is any information from our home base.' Lorraine picked up her mobile phone.

'Okay, thanks, Lorraine. I'm going in for a shower. Shall we meet say in an hour? We could then go to the plant to analyse the samples?'

'Yes Robert, of course,' she smiled at him, and he kissed her lightly on her cheek. 'An hour yes?' Robert nodded and headed off.

Lorraine needed to clean up too, she felt grubby from walking about the old town and the flaking, crumbling buildings. She returned to her room, checked all the doors and windows were closed and walked into the bathroom, and ran the taps to fill the bathtub and returned to the bedroom. She sat on the bed and took her mobile phone and called Debbie.

'Hello Debbie, it's Lorraine. How are you?

'Hello, Lorraine. Good, how are things going with you?'

'I'm okay. I'm out in Equatorial Guinea still, how's Jessica?'

'Ah, she's good. She enjoys her food.' Debbie laughed. 'She doesn't leave me alone when I pop in each day.'

'Thank you, Debbie, I do appreciate your help. Could you tell me if you've received any samples from Equatorial Guinea, please?'

'Yes. Apart from the standard ones we receive from the production plant, we've had a flurry of other samples coming through, but they are labelled as clothing samples! Do you know why?'

'Yes, there was an incident out here, and I think Hugh sampled them and sent them back.'

'Yes. Indeed, they do appear to have been signed by him.'

'Do you have any results yet?'

'It's been difficult to determine. They are coming through a little worse for wear. There has been sample damage, and the DNA doesn't appear complete. Either these samples have been tampered with, or they have been contaminated with something. Certainly, the gas chromatography shows that they are very acidic. But let me finish these and I'll get back to you.'

'Thanks, Debbie.'

'Oh, Lorraine?'

'Yes.'

'I think something is going on here. I think Hugh's in some big trouble.'

'Why? What do you mean?'

'The finance department has been audited, and there are some irregularities on Hugh's corporate credit card. The finance director is after him. He had to field off some difficult questions with the auditors. And Theresa says that Arthur's very worried about Hugh, he's not answering calls.'

'Okay thanks, Debbie.'

'Lorraine, please be careful out there, you know how hot-headed he can be.'

'Yes don't I know it!' replied Lorraine.

'Bye.' Debbie's last comments hung in Lorraine's mind. She thought about Hugh's attack, and she suddenly felt deeply melancholy and lonely. Lorraine started to cry. None of this was meant to happen. Just a week ago life was fun.

Right, she thought. *Be brave. Smarten up. We'll get the samples analysed this afternoon, and tomorrow was going to be another day.*

Lorraine picked up her mobile phone again and opened her Outlook application. She started to write an email. It was a factual, accurate and truthful account of what Lorraine had witnessed over the last forty-eight hours. Lorraine reflected on how although the idea that Hugh had proposed about following Robert had initially been fun, and she thought of benefit to the organisation with the publicity of the Digester going live, events had taken a turn when she had arrived in Equatorial Guinea.

She was aware that her visit was not "official", and as a senior manager she had to be seen to be doing the right thing. Her career was also on the line. She was worried that she could be regarded as being complicit if there was no evidence of her attempting to addresses the issues that were materialising.

Lorraine put her corporate "head" on. Robert probably knew far more than was healthy, she trusted him undoubtedly, but Robert's view of the organisation, its flaws and contamination issue first hand started to worry Lorraine. He was after all a writer, an author, a researcher and this information could materialise, in a book, an article or even an interview.

It was a risk to her company and also to Lorraine's career. The company should have visibility of the whole situation. But she could also see the impact that the bacterial contamination could have on the environment. People, like Robert, needed to spread that message, while companies still needed to keep their secrets. She had a conflict of interest that she was having trouble reconciling.

But Lorraine also wanted to make clear all the issues she had witnessed, and although she still wasn't sure what Hugh's aims were, he had caused a lot of trouble. By the time Lorraine had finished, the email was over three-hundred words.

Lorraine took a deep breath, slowly exhaled then pressed send. She had addressed it to Arthur.Tate@GM-Agrotech.com. The one person she thought would see things rationally and be in a position to act.

She then went to the bathroom for a relaxing hot soak. While she soaked in the warm, steamy, perfumed haze, the email server rifled through the emails and forwarded the email to the intended recipient, and one other person.

#

'Hugh, it's all going pear-shaped. You have to realise this. The samples taken from the gyres show extreme levels of tetrahydride acid and xylene, and the level of micro-plastics is a disaster. The plastic sinks as it loses buoyancy and these micro-plastics are an even greater problem than the original waste, not just for marine life at the surface but at all depths. These will get into the food chain faster than the large plastics. At least the large stuff can be contained.'

'Okay, Adam. It will be improved. This is a test environment. You can't deny that it's been a success, we've digested about a thousand tons of plastic at sea, at source within a month.'

'But Hugh, this is real life, not a laboratory. It's been a complete waste of time. You've already said that there are better genetically modified bacteria that don't produce such harmful by-products. What is the purpose of all this? The pollution, the cost, the deaths?'

'The deaths had nothing to do with this. It was a storm.'

'Hugh, you can fool your team and pay off the harbour masters and the press, but I know the truth. There's no point trying to lie to me.'

Hugh looked frustrated. 'At worst it was an unfortunate accident. But Adam, the point, the whole point of this was to demonstrate how good bacteria could be to digest these ocean gyres. Tonnes of plastic wash down streams and rivers and end up in the sea. The ability to spray them and make them harmless would demonstrate that GM Agro-Tech was an innovative company and it would make us both successful and rich and clean up the planet.'

'Sure, you have a neat product, but you haven't really thought this through. You got me involved to monitor samples and give you real data, and advice. But you haven't taken any of it in on board. None of it. Even after the incident here and the impact at Ngaba village downstream, you've just ploughed on without thinking of the consequences. Hugh, have you ever considered what would happen to all that E. coli in the sea when the plastic is broken down? Where does it go? What about the Xylene that's toxic and killing the fish?'

'Adam, I've heard enough. This is one isolated patch, any bacteria or plastics' by-products will be diluted by the oceans.'

'No that's exactly what people think when we flush plastic down the drains, it all ends up in the sea, diluted in massive oceans. But all this waste is piling up, and now your solution is killing the marine species at sea and on waterways inland.'

'Enough!' Hugh barked. 'I think you forget who funds your laboratories and field trips. Without the funds, I provide you wouldn't be able to go off on these maritime jollies of yours!'

Adam's face was getting visibly red with frustration with Hugh. *Why won't this supposedly smart scientist just listen?* he thought.

Hugh's mobile phone interrupted his rant.

'Hugh, where are you?' It was Arthur on the line.

Hugh's eyes rolled. *Will the old man never give up?*

'Hello, Arthur, I'm here in Equatorial Guinea, checking on last-minute preparation for go-live. Why are you calling? Do you need me for something?'

'We have matters here we need to resolve, I have been trying to call you. I have the finance director here, and I still need to talk with you about our contract with Butler Oil & Gas. I have a conference call you need to contribute to. It's important that we all agree…'

'Arthur, I don't have time for this,' Hugh cut in. 'I'm trying to sort out plans for our future here. We should just tell Jim we do not agree to his terms. He'll come around eventually and give us a better deal.' There was a pause, and Hugh heard Jim's voice on the phone.

'Hello Hugh, it's Jim here. As Arthur said, he has called you on the conference line. There are urgent matters that we need to resolve.' It now became apparent that this was the conference call! Hugh became flushed with embarrassment and rage.

'Look, Jim, I'm sorry there is nothing to discuss with you.'

'Actually yes there is,' Jim replied. 'But if it's any comfort, Hugh, you were right. Butler Oil & Gas cannot do without GM Agro-Tech.'

'I'm glad you've come around to my way of thinking, Jim. See, Arthur, what did I tell you? Now I hope we can all agree on better terms.' Hugh was feeling confident again, back in control of the situation.

Jim continued as if Hugh hadn't spoken. '… So with the agreement of Arthur and the board, we have started procedures to take over GM Agro-Tech and make it a subsidiary of Butler Oil & Gas, a Gene Modification Division, if you like. Since you first alerted us to the commercial risks at our conference over a month ago, we have made strides to consolidate the situation and secure our operations. A takeover will allow us to operate with Arthur and it gives him space, to manage his other business activities in research and attend to scientific matters. We've tried to include you, Hugh, but you've always been too busy and evasive.'

'I've been trying to tell you, Hugh,' said Arthur. 'I think this is best for GM Agro-Tech and Butler Oil & Gas. It's better all round.'

Hugh was raging. 'Arthur, you are weak, a traitor to the company. Peter must be turning in his grave to see what you have turned this company into. I guess you want me to return and get this mess sorted out for you now?' Arthur took a sharp intake of breath. Unknown to Hugh this comment had hurt Arthur like a stake through the heart. And Jim noticed the paleness in Arthur's face.

Jim cut in again. 'Well, actually no, Hugh. I don't think you realise how much Arthur has protected you and supported all your initiatives. Arthur has signed off the financial audit report at a great personal loss to save you from financial impropriety hearings. But both Arthur and I have decided that the new company needs to distance itself from you.'

'Why? What do you mean distance itself from me?' Hugh shouted.

'We have received evidence of some activities that you have been up to in the name of the company. I understand that there is a criminal prosecution heading our way. Something to do with your using genetically modified material, GM Agro-Tech products, illegally and irresponsibly, in the open sea, leading directly to the deaths of fifteen fishermen.'

'What happened here, Hugh? What did you get involved in?' asked Arthur, his voice pained.

'None of this is true, uncle. This is not true. Who is raising the criminal prosecution? Who? I'll see them in court.'

'Well actually, it's GM Agro-Tech, supported by Butler Oil & Gas,' Jim replied. 'The new organisation cannot be seen to endorse illegal use of GM material outside the work we are trying to do with digesters. Hugh, we know you took stock from secure stores and used it in an uncontrolled environment, that you paid men to spray and measure the plastic gyres, leading to their deaths. And then you attempted to cover it all up. Hugh, you are no longer employed by GM Agro-Tech, and I'd suggest as a friend that you reach out for a good lawyer.'

'Friend? Jim go fuck yourself. You to Arthur, both of you go fuck yourselves!' Hugh shouted at the phone and hung up. He felt his blood boiling as if his head was about to explode. He slammed his mobile phone onto the floor, watching the screen smash into tiny, plastic pieces across the polished granite surface.

#

Robert and Lorraine arrived at the production facility. There were no guards, and the gates were open. They drove in and parked the car. There was another car parked in the car park, and they could see the lights on in the office at the top of the gantry.

'Robert, let's go directly to the lab, not to the office.'

'Sure.'

Robert followed Lorraine to the laboratory. She turned the lights on and powered up the two analysers.

They heard muffled voices from the office above them, but they couldn't make out the conversation.

'Well, you can't be surprised. You've acted with total nonchalance and disregard of your industry from the start. You're a fucking loose cannon. I don't know why I got involved with this.'

'Arthur is blind. He's only interested in his own little world.'

'And you're not?' Hugh paused after Adam's comment. *'Let's try and bring Adam back onside with this, he's the only one who can help,'* he thought.

141

'Adam stay with me on this. You have done well ensuring the gyre was not found, spinning the algae bloom propaganda, and paying the harbour master off, but we have time to turn this around.'

'Hugh you've gone too far. If your company is prosecuting you, I can't be around for that. It would destroy me.'

'If I go down, you're coming with me. You've milked my company for years.'

'I've worked for this funding! I've supported almost every discovery with well-worded reports for you. I've monitored the gyre, downplayed the marine damage and the massive amount of micro-plastics building up. We were ready for publication until the deaths, and then you said wait a while.'

'Give it time and help me and this will die down and then publish.'

'It's not going to happen now, Hugh.'

'Okay. If that's how you feel. You know that you are indicted in this? Some would even accuse you of attempted murder.'

'Why would you say that?'

'Well, you got the Howdon girl involved, and she ended up getting injured on the island. You knew the risks, and the chance she'd be hurt.'

'Thanks. Thanks a lot! You insisted that I get her out here to improve your publicity, and you arranged to put that bacterial strain on the gyre.'

'Yes, but to take her on a fucking sailing trip to the island you dumb shit, after what it did to those men.'

'There was no way of knowing that Juan was going to head that way.'

#

In the laboratory, Lorraine was about to start the analysis.

'Robert, I need to connect that CO_2 cylinder here, to replace the empty one, but I can't get the pressure reducing valve off. It's too tight. Could you do this for me please?

'Sure,' Robert replied happy to oblige. He gripped the reducing valve tight and used more effort than he expected to loosen the lid.

'I'll add more phosphate buffer to this tank, while you do that.'

Lorraine filled the buffer tank with a new bottle of phosphate buffered saline, and Robert unscrewed the valve. He disconnected the old portable CO2 cylinder and stood it on the floor. He connected the new barrel, tightened the pressure, reducing valve on and opened the tap on the valve. Lorraine started the analysis.

'This shouldn't take long,' she said.

Robert turned to watch. As he moved, he caught the freestanding cylinder with his foot, and accidentally kicked the empty cylinder over. It clanked onto the floor and rolled a couple of times, coming to a halt next to a metal table with another loud metallic clunk.

#

'Anyway, there is only one way out now,' Hugh said.

'What way is that?' Adam was aware that his career was on the brink of annihilation if his corruption around sampling and scientific findings were to be made public. His association with Hugh and GM Agro-Tech was becoming toxic. He needed to distance himself from the company and Hugh if he was to survive.

'Getting our two nemeses to remain quiet is the only way we will survive this.'

'Who do you mean?'

'Lorraine Bellamy and Robert Howdon.'

'I don't know her, and Robert Howdon is Jane's father, the writer. What would this achieve?'

'He's made some claims against my company, and he's here visiting his daughter, you know the one you put in the hospital! Lorraine was supposed to bring him out here nearer the production date; having his daughter here as well would have raised awareness and publicity, but her accident brought everything forward. He was on our side. Now I'm not so sure. Lorraine has information, but we need to get to her before it all gets back to Jim…'

They were interrupted by a metallic clunk somewhere below them.

Hugh looked at Adam. They walked out of the office and looked over the gantry rail, down towards the laboratory. They could see Lorraine and Robert below them.

They had no idea what the two below them might have heard. Hugh decided to play it cool, and let them lead the conversation.

Hugh stepped forward and called over the gantry.

'Lorraine, Robert, would you both like to join me up here? There are a few things I think we should discuss.'

Lorraine and Robert looked up at Hugh and then looked at each other.

'We'll be with you in a second, let me just finish this analysis,' called up Lorraine

'I don't trust him, Robert,' Lorraine whispered. 'We need to be careful, he threatened me this morning when you knocked.'

'Really?' Robert said surprised. 'Did he stay over?'

'No, nothing like that, of course not. He walked into my room this morning when the doors were open to the garden, you know before breakfast.'

'Are you coming guys?' Hugh shouted again.

'Don't worry, Lorraine I'm here. There is two of us, we'll be fine,' Robert whispered grabbing her hand.

The ticker tape printed out and Lorraine tore it off. She glanced at it and placed it in the pocket of her slacks.

'We're coming,' she shouted.

They climbed the steps up to the gantry. Robert was surprised to see two people on the gantry. He instantly recognised Adam. 'Professor Wilmsford, what are you doing here? How are you involved with this?'

Adam smiled and raised his eyebrows at Robert, who turned to face Hugh. 'Are you Hugh? I think we met at the hospital.'

'Yes, this is Hugh,' said Lorraine.

Hugh responded with a smile and a nod. 'Yes, that was me at the hospital.'

'Why didn't you introduce yourself to me?' asked Robert.

'You didn't know me at that point, there was no point confusing things.'

'No point confusing things? My daughter was in that hospital because of you and your company.' Robert turned to Adam. 'And Prof, what are you doing here? Did you have any involvement with Jane's accident?'

Adam shrugged and said, 'No, apart from getting her on this trip.'

Robert continued. 'But you were the man Bartho called Senor Adam, the man who paid his men? And I saw you pay off the harbour master and throw the boat keys into the water at the marina.'

Adam suddenly felt trapped. Robert knew far more than Hugh had suggested, and he didn't like the way he was becoming implicated in this whole mess.

Adam remained silent, although he and Hugh glanced at each other.

'Have you seen the corporate email this afternoon, Hugh?' Lorraine asked. 'It was all about the merger of GM Agro-Tech and Butler Oil & Gas.' Lorraine had read some corporate emails while waiting for her bath to fill, and an email with a "celebratory theme" was circulated about the merger of the two companies. The board listed did not include Hugh.

Hugh was crestfallen that this news had been released so quickly, and his face showed his disappointment at Lorraine knowing already.

'Yes, thank you Lorraine, I am aware of it, and we have been planning this for some time. It makes perfect sense as…'

'But Hugh, you are not part of the new arrangement, are you?' Lorraine continued. 'In fact, a memo sent to me and my team after the corporate message directly requested that no staff had dealings with you, as allegations were being made against you and you were no longer an employee.' Lorraine was bluffing, other than the message confirming concern over Hugh's roll in the illegal use of corporate facilities. 'So I ought to be asking you what you are doing here since you no longer work for us.'

'And what about you, Lorraine, what are you doing here? After hours, with a reporter. Spying maybe? It all looks very suspicious,' Hugh smiled.

'Enough Hugh, we want some answers,' said Robert. 'People have died. You are both involved in this, and my daughter got messed up in this somehow, too. What the hell is going on? What have you done, Hugh?'

'Robert, don't overreact,' Hugh stepped forward. 'You can't make an omelette without cracking an egg, and I'm afraid some eggs were cracked here. It was unfortunate that those fishermen died in the storm.'

'Don't give us that rubbish, Hugh,' said Lorraine. 'We know there wasn't a storm, and we know that you were using one of the early strains, IS-23, on that gyre. That's what injured Bartho and killed those other men.'

'Shit!' said Adam. 'She knows.'

'Shut up, you idiot.' Hugh sneered at Adam and turned to face Lorraine. 'You have no proof of that, it's just a rumour, and GM Agro-Tech was not involved.'

'There was no storm that day, the records show clear skies and mild weather,' said Robert.

'Hugh, you had several batches of the test GM bacteria strains IS-23 shipped to Bata, although the production plant was using IS-48,' said Lorraine. 'The boats that you used to spray the island were registered to GM Agro-Tech. They even had the company logo on the windscreen.'

'And they were registered and tracked on the Port Bata commercial ship tracking system,' added Robert.

'Your involvement in this is obvious.' There was a note of triumph in Lorraine's voice.

Hugh glared at Lorraine. 'You bitch! You've been waiting for this moment, haven't you? But you have no idea!' Hugh paused and stood firmly looking at them both.

'I should have killed you this morning when I had the chance.'

'You've over-stepped the mark now,' Robert said, putting himself between Hugh and Lorraine. 'You're in serious trouble, and I think the police should know.' Robert pulled out his mobile phone.

'I don't think so!' Hugh shouted. He lunged forward to grab Robert's phone. Robert pulled his arm back and stepped away placing his phone back promptly into his pocket. Hugh stumbled forward and pushed his shoulder into Robert's groin. Robert lunged onto the guardrail. Hugh fell heavily onto the floor.

Lorraine looked at Adam, unsure of what his response was going to be. She stepped slowly towards Robert, feeling for her mobile phone in her bag.

'Lorraine, I don't think you should make that call,' said Adam. 'You don't know what you are doing, this could destroy you and your company.'

'No Adam, enough is enough, we have to end this,' Lorraine replied. Adam dived forward and knocked her bag out of her hand. It fell through the handrail to the floor below the gantry.

Robert regained his balance, turned and saw what had happened. 'Adam, stop,' he shouted. 'Keep out of this. It's not your problem.'

'I think it is,' sneered Hugh from the floor of the gantry. 'Money, Robert, it's money that motivates Adam. All his shiny new technology doesn't come cheap.'

'It was Adam who arranged for Jane to sail into the gyre. He arranged for Bartho and the men to spray the island, and he paid off the harbour master to inform the press of the storm at sea.'

Adam starred at Hugh in disbelief.

Robert glared at Adam. 'Did you? You bastard, you fucking bastard.' He lunged at Adam. Adam tried to get out of his way, but the full force of Robert's fist came down on his skull, near the base of his neck.

Adam fell forward and groaned. But he got up quickly and reached for a metal stool. Now standing, he swung it around his head and caught Robert's shoulder. Robert was forced back through the main door and stumbled down the top metal step leading down to the digester. He grabbed the handrail and winced with pain. He looked back over his shoulder and saw Hugh getting up and heading for Lorraine. 'Lorraine! Watch out!'

Lorraine looked around and saw Hugh coming towards her. She backed away and descended a set of stairs on the other side of the gantry leading to the test laboratories below, and ran out through the double doors labelled "Exit". She headed towards her car. Hugh saw the path she had taken and followed her.

Adam swung at Robert again and hit the handrail, dealing a glancing blow to Robert's hand.

'Robert, you need to know that I wanted Jane's class to find the gyre and maximise publicity. That's what Hugh and I wanted, but that stupid Juan ran the boat aground, so he deserves what he gets.'

'You're despicable. You could have killed him and Jane and all those other kids.'

'That would have been a shame, but I'd rather that than lose everything I've worked for.' Adam swung the stool again.

Robert continued down the stairs and stepped into the viscous mud at the bottom of the staircase. He struggled for a moment, then pulled his foot out of the mud and stumbled away as quickly as he could. Adam stomped down the stairs after him.

Robert looked for Lorraine but couldn't see her. Now on firmer ground, he ran along the side of building towards the dam, looking around him in search of something to use as a weapon. He so wanted to beat the living daylights out of that bastard, Adam, who had tried to hurt Jane and her friends. Just imagining that she could have ended up like Bartho or worse scared him and energised him for revenge.

Robert heard some noise in the mud behind him. He could see Adam through the jungle foliage. He hurried to the dam steps and started to climb them. The steps were slippery and overgrown, and the dim light of the bulb barely lit them.

Adam peered through the darkness. The dim light by the dam wall was just sufficient for Adam to see a glint from the zip in Robert's jacket as he scaled the dark stairway. Adam changed direction and headed for the dam.

Lorraine saw her car and headed for it, walking quickly over the uneven ground, and occasionally stumbling on the bumpy gravel road. What was she thinking? In her eagerness to get away, she had left her bag behind. It had fallen to the ground floor below the gantry, along with her mobile phone and all its contents including her car keys.

Lorraine fumbled in her pockets, for something, anything! She didn't see the club-sized log swing through the air behind her. It came crashing down on the side of her head. The pain, Lorraine let out a stifled scream that ended before her crumpled form fell lifeless onto the muddy ground. 'You deserve that you bitch. I should have done that two days ago when you first turned up!' Hugh sneered victoriously.

On the dam, above the tree line, the twilight blue sky provided sufficient light for Robert to follow the narrow path along the wall to the river. Robert thought he heard a woman's scream in the near distance, but it cut off suddenly. Turning towards the sound, he strained to hear further noises. But the only sound was that of the gurgle of water falling over the weir onto the idle plastic shredding machine. *Was that Lorraine?* he thought. *What the hell is going on? How desperate are these two?* Robert stood there, uncertain. Should he return to help Lorraine? Was he even sure it was Lorraine?

He stepped carefully along the narrow path at the top of the dam, along the water's edge towards the shredder and the other set of stairs. He thought if he quietly and covertly backtracked he could find Lorraine, get the car and they could get themselves out of here and call the police.

Suddenly the lights next to the shredder came on, and the machinery started up, with a deep cranking sound. The hum became a roar as the mechanism sped up. Out of the shadows from the top of the steps, Adam stepped into the full bright light.

Adam looked menacing. He stood defiantly by the steps blocking Robert's escape.

'Adam, let me get past and let it go. It's Hugh who caused this problem. Let him deal with it and suffer the consequences.' Robert spoke calmly, but he was seething and could have easily killed the man on the spot.

'No way Robert, you know far too much. You'd blab to the press or write a fancy story for money while Hugh and I served time,' Adam also spoke calmly. He moved slowly towards Robert as he spoke. 'There's no way I'm having you and Lorraine ruin my career when I can end it all.'

He paused. 'Now.'

He lifted a large monkey wrench that he had been holding down by his leg and raised it across his chest in both hands.

'Time to say goodbye, Robert.' Adam took a swing at Robert, who instinctively ducked, but Robert's foot slid on the algae-covered concrete path, and he fell into the damp ferns at the water's edge. His leg went into the plastic and water, less than a metre below him. The plastic bobbed with the ripples.

Adam swung again at Robert's leg, and this time made contact with his right ankle. Robert howled in pain, but quickly brought his left leg across and caught Adam's leg, throwing him off balance. Adam's deck shoes slipped on the wet concrete. He dropped the wrench and fell into the river. He sank below the layer of plastic; plastic debris quickly filled the hole Adam had left. Robert paused to glance in the water, nothing? *Perhaps he's really gone,* Robert thought.

As he turned away, Adam lurched out of the water and landed an arm on to the riverbank. He grabbed a tree root; his other arm came out and lunged onto the land next to Robert's feet. Robert turned to move, but Adam grabbed his ankle. He fell backwards, hard, into a tree root on the bank. Using both arms now, Adam pulled himself out of the water and rested on all fours, staring at Robert like a panther waiting to pounce on his prey. Robert got up as quickly as he could and headed towards the steps. Adam lunged again, spinning Robert around. This time Robert was able to use the momentum of the turn to deliver a punch to Adam's jaw.

The punch and the force behind it caught Adam by surprise and twisted his body around, and he stumbled backwards. His body fell hard onto the edge of the bank with his torso hanging from the bank a metre above the plastic flotsam, with just his legs below the water line. The rotating metal gears continued to pull plastic from the river into its mechanisms, with regular taps and thuds.

Adam, hanging over the bank, turned his body in an attempt to stand. He tried to pull himself up, but he couldn't get a grip on the slimy concrete edge. He put his left arm below the water and found something substantial to give him something to push against.

As he pushed and started to get up, he felt his sleeve catch on something below the surface; his arm began to lift. This assisted him further to stand, as he was almost standing on the bank, on one bent knee, his arm then began to sink. It was caught on the rotary gearing mechanism that pulled plastic into the shredder. Adam suddenly, realised what had happened. He panicked and tried to pull his arm backwards. There was an audible rip as his shirtsleeve came away. Adam looked towards Robert, a menacing smile on his face. Adam thought he was free.

But the rotary mechanism continued to turn. The grip of the blades turned and tightened around his wrist pulling him down. Robert saw the horror on Adam's face, as he frantically tried to get his trapped arm out. Robert had no idea what was happening. He felt equally helpless but relieved that Adam could not pursue him.

The rotor pulled Adam's body downwards into the shredder as the gears continued to turn. The grip tightened further, and the mechanism began to labour under the stress. Its movement was less regular, and the pitch of the motor rose to a scream.

Robert stepped forward and could see Adam's predicament. Adam's whole arm was now in the shredder, up to his shoulder. 'Please turn it off, stop it!' Adam pleaded as Robert approached.

Robert took a second to react; then he moved quickly. 'I'll go and get some help,' and ran past him, down the steps toward the gantry and the other buildings.

Behind him, Robert could hear Adam begging and screaming in pain. The blades were biting into his flesh, against the resistance his shoulder was generating.

Robert looked for a power source to isolate, to stop the shredder. He passed under the gantry and along the digester, where Jim had brought him.

He walked the length of the digester until he reached the submarine-type door. It was ajar.

Robert peered in. Jim had said this door was always firmly closed. He leant in further.

From the shadows, a figure leapt forward and pushed Robert hard in the middle of his back. Robert fell forward into the digester. He turned to hear the hinges creak as the door closed, the door wheel turned and the door was firmly shut behind him.

'Who is that? Let me out!' Robert called out. There was no response. Robert listened, he could still hear the shredder working, and Adam calling out in a shaky, panicked voice.

'Let me out. Hugh, Lorraine? Someone, let me out. We have to save Adam. He's stuck in the shredder, we need to turn the power off.'

Turning away from the digester, Hugh headed up to the gantry to start the process running. He heard Robert shout something out. The bookworm was probably panicking and begging to be let out. That was never going to happen. Hugh smirked. At the gantry, he pulled two of the breakers up into position. The dull thud of the switches being turned on, and the subsequent increase in power, made all the lights momentarily brighten. He pressed the start button for the digester process to begin. The motor of the digester twitched into action and slowly increased in speed, accompanied by the gentle hum of the motor.

In the distance, towards the dam, he thought he heard a man's scream. It caused him to pause. Was that a man or an animal? It sounded familiar, but then it faded, and Hugh carried on. He activated the pellet line to the digester and turned on the water pumps.

'Right,' he laughed. 'That should sort him out!'

Robert called out again. Still, there was no response. In the distance, he thought he heard a humming sound. He strained to make it out. Was it a vehicle or another generator? Then something clicked loudly, and the impeller in the middle of the tank twitched into action. It started to slowly rotate.

Robert fumbled in his pocket for his mobile phone. He brought it out and looked on it for any signal. It wasn't surprising that there was no signal as he was within a metal tank, the battery was also low at twenty-five per cent. He opened the torch app to provide some light. Shining the torch around, Robert could see the huge impellor in the centre, and several probes sticking into the side of the tank. Robert knew from Jim's tour that these were for monitoring the digesting process, the PH, oxygen and probably water levels. Looking around he also noticed inlets for growth media, and below there were pipes to take products out to the separation tanks.

But how to get out? The impeller had picked up speed slightly, and the two-metre blades could soon do some damage if they made contact with him. There was barely a metre clearance around the impeller to the side of the tank. Robert could feel the air pulling his trouser legs as each blade passed. The clicking was getting louder. Then it stopped.

As Robert strained to listen, suddenly millions of pellets began to cascade out of a large pipe above his head, like cockroaches storming out of a drain.

Robert quickly considered his options. He looked at the top of the impeller shaft, but couldn't see any welds, although a seal was evident. He looked further around to see how it was powered. By torchlight, he saw that the whole disc at the top of the impeller was turning. The only way this could occur would be by a magnetic drive connection, an ingenious technology that avoided having any seals connected to the outside, keeping the contents of the tank protected.

Weighing up his options, Robert jumped onto the impeller. It had sped up slightly, and he felt giddy standing on two of the four-impeller paddles.

As it turned Robert moved his weight back and forth starting to rock it. Each time he rocked, he felt a little lateral movement, like the start of a pendulum swing. He did this again and again, and on the sixth revolution, the impeller rocked so violently that it came away from the grip of the magnetic drive plate.

The impeller came crashing down, with a loud metallic clang that resonated for some time. Robert was pinned under the shaft, squashed against the side of the tank, with the full weight of the impeller blade on his foot and ankle.

He was exhausted, and wet. Wet? He looked to see that the inlet pipe had started to pour water into the tank.

As the water poured in, the pellets collecting on the bottom of the tank started to act like quicksand. He felt himself sinking. Robert didn't want to drown; he needed to do something, and fast. As he slowly sank into the quagmire, he felt the gap between himself and the impeller increasing. He was able to free himself from the wedged paddles. He dropped low behind the shaft and scampered out from below the impeller paddles. The weight of the plastic pellets continued to drag him down. He needed some help to counteract these negative forces.

How can I stop this? Robert thought. His familiarity with process control and his understanding of feedback mechanisms gave him an idea. If he broke one of the control probes, the system should crash and come to a halt. Robert smiled. He clambered up and stood on the mound of pellets that slowly crumbled below him, and stepped on more as they continued to flood in. He stretched to reach the glass probes. They remained just beyond his reach. Robert removed a shoe and attempted to smash one of them. After several attempts, as he started to sink again, the probe then smashed. In the distance, an alarm sounded, and he smiled. The loss of the PH probe should be important enough in the process to raise the alarm and halt the flow of pellets and water.

However, although the alarm sounded, the pellets continued to tumble in, and water continued to pour. Robert stepped higher on the plastic mound as it grew ever higher. Water had reached Robert's chest, and his head was near the top of the digester.

He was out of ideas.

#

Adam found the pull on his arms intolerable, unbearable. The pain of his ligaments being pulled apart was torture. The wheeled mechanism tore at his skin, it bit in, deeper and deeper, until it was grating on his bones.

'No. Help! Please help!' Adam whimpered in the darkness. For what seemed like an eternity the motor chugged, unable to make progress, constantly pulling against Adam's torso. The lights down the steps dimmed and brightened with every high-pitched turn of the mechanism until suddenly he heard the distant thud of Hugh turning on a breaker and the lights grew brighter, much brighter.

The motor was re-energised, and the mechanism ramped up, with renewed vigour; it gored at Adam's arm with heightened malice. The device clamped harder and clawed deeper, now scouring the bone of all flesh. Adam was feeling nauseous and close to passing out.

In a single powerful jolt, the mechanism tore through Adam's arm at the shoulder and freed him from the torment. Adam screamed an ear-piercing scream, from the intense pain, and then felt a strange sense of relief. He was free.

The relief that Adam felt was short lived. Blood pumped in regular surges from his severed shoulder arteries. His body soon started to cool, and Adam slowly slipped into a deep sleep, one he would never awaken from.

Adam's lifeless body toppled further back, deep into the mechanism's gears. His shoulder, chest then head entered the churning metallic abyss. The motors started to choke, and the gears moved sporadically. The engine screamed again, and Adam's body was pulled deeper into the ears. It shuddered and shook as the gears attempted to turn, paused and turned again. The lights flickered and dimmed, flickered and dimmed again. In the distance, breakers failed with a loud bang and all power was lost.

#

The pellets continued to fall in around Robert, and water continued to pour. Robert tried to keep above the water line, which was now at his neck. His feet were on the top of the impeller shaft, but they kept sliding off. Robert was beginning to think of his wife, his daughter, his life… trying to survive as now with his neck bent, and his head tight to the roof of the digester, he struggled to breathe.

Suddenly there was an ear-piercing scream in the distance. There was a pause, and then a loud bang. The lights outside dimmed, shone brighter and were then extinguished. All the machinery stopped. The pellets stopped flowing into the digester, and the water level slowly began to drop.

#

Hugh picked up two heavy billycans full of fuel and carried them to his car. He threw them into the boot and started the engine. His wheels spun in the mud, and the car fishtailed until it gained traction on the gravel.

Hugh skidded out of the production facility at speed. He hurtled down the jungle path, onto the mountain roads towards the marina at Port Bata.

As he headed lower, he realised the time. It was nearing dawn, and the sky was beginning to brighten. Hugh was focused on his goal. He realised that now his opponents were gone, he must destroy all the evidence. He had a plan and had to complete it. No more distractions! What was Lorraine thinking? Traitors! What was wrong with the world? Why couldn't everyone see the genius he was? Given the chance, and time, he could perform miracles.

Nearing the marina, he could see the remaining boat he had hired for the gyre spraying. If only the world could see what he had done, breaking down plastic at source in the sea. He had shown that plastics could be digested; the trillions of plastic items in the sea could be controlled and destroyed, bringing an end to the problem. Why was everyone against him?

Hugh felt embittered. He loaded the billycans onto the small flat-bottomed boat. He started up the engines, and as the exhaust spluttered, headed out of the harbour to the last known location of the gyre.

An hour later, Hugh could see a low-lying mist marking the location of the gyre ahead. He could smell the gyre. It was much worse than he remembered from one of his very infrequent visits. The water appeared red and turbid as the bow wave cut through the calm ocean.

The closer he approached, he saw that more of the surface was littered with dead marine life in various states of decay. He saw turtles, seagulls and fish of all sizes. Tuna, Bonita, Bass and, surprisingly, dolphins.

This shocked Hugh. He didn't understand. Surely the bacteria couldn't have done this? This was a good thing, the saviour, the new hope! Not a danger, not even more deadly than plastic itself.

Hugh pulled the boat next to the edge of the gyre. The acrid smell was overwhelming. His eyes watered and he coughed. He placed a glove he found over his nose and mouth and scrambled ashore with the first billycan. He threw it about the island and discarded the spent container on the gyre and stumbled back across the uneven surface to the boat. He spread the second billycan across the remaining area of the island.

Relieved, he jumped back into the boat and started the engine. Once the rhythmic tut-tut of the engine had begun, he opened a box of matches and lit some paper in the bottom of the boat. It caught readily.

Hugh threw the paper ashore, and the petrol fumes caught instantly. He was surprised at how fast the fire grew; within seconds the whole plastic gyre was in flames. Feeling the intense heat, he put the motor into drive to get away.

The engine stalled.

Hugh tried to start it again and again, but the bacteria had already begun to dissolve the plastic intake hose, and the motor could not run without overheating and stalling.

On the gyre, the flammable xylene by-product of the bacterial digestion had reached its flash point temperate of thirty degrees centigrade and started to burn, the flames and heat quickly intensified. Soon the boat and Hugh were engulfed by the fire.

Hugh screamed as the water, the plastic and his skin bubbled, twisted and burnt in unison, as one in the inferno. After several agonising seconds, he fell silent and still.

From Port Bata, sunrise highlighted the plume of dense smoke that rose high on the horizon.

#

The calm morning was broken by the shrill regular beat of ambulance and police car sirens as they headed out of the Police Station at the harbour towards the mountains, heading to a production facility where some injuries had been reported. A man named Jerry Hawkins had called emergency services at four-thirty am when he received an automated alert indicating a system failure at the production facility at San Carlos. He investigated and reported a fatality and someone suffering from concussion.

'Lorraine, Lorraine can you hear me?' Jerry said. He had arrived at the production facility and seen Lorraine's car. As he had approached it, he saw Lorraine lying on the ground.

Her head was marred by a bloody gash that had matted her hair, and there was a huge lump at the back of her head.

She was breathing shallowly, and he tried to revive her.

'Lorraine, can you hear me?' He asked again. He sat on the ground next to her and laid her head in his lap.

'Uhh, ouch, it hurts.' Lorraine slowly responded, rolling over then attempted to be sick. She was feeling nauseous and horribly dizzy. Her head ached, and she felt tired and cold.

'There, don't move, just lay still. An ambulance is on its way.'

'Thank you, Jerry,' she replied, trying to smile. 'Where is Robert? He was here, have you seen him? My God, Hugh and Adam were here as well. Are they still here? Be careful, Jerry.' Lorraine became tense and looked around.

'Don't you worry. There's no one else here. I don't know where the others are. But don't you worry. Let's sort you out first.' He stroked her forehead. Then he bent forward and kissed her. Lorraine closed her eyes and smiled.

Soon a police car and an ambulance arrived. The ambulance pulled up next to the car, and two paramedics came over to Jerry and Lorraine.

'Senorita, what happened here? How are you?' the paramedic asked.

157

'My head hurts. I think I was hit, I... I passed out.' The paramedics chatted in Spanish and one brought over a stretcher and a neck brace.

'How many fingers am I holding up, Senorita?'

'Five,' she said, correctly.

'Where are we, Senorita?' they asked her. She couldn't remember the actual location, but she said, 'An operations plant in Port Bata, Equatorial Guinea.' They looked at Jerry, who nodded.

They strapped a neck brace on and constrained Lorraine's head and neck, took her pulse and checked her pupils.

'Senor, you know her?' one of the paramedics asked Jerry.

'Yes, I know her.'

'What is her name and nationality?'

'Her name is Lorraine Bellamy. She is British,' he answered.

'And yours, Senor? Senor Bellamy, is it?'

'No, it's Jerry Hawkins. I'm a friend.' Jerry and Lorraine exchanged glances and smiled.

The paramedics entered details on a form and placed it on Lorraine's stomach as they stretchered her to the ambulance.

'Jerry,' she called. Jerry walked over to her in the ambulance. She looked concerned.

'Everything's fine,' he said, to soothe her. 'You go with the ambulance now, Lorraine. I'll speak with the police and meet you at the hospital. You go and get checked out.' He held her hand and leant down and kissed her forehead. 'I'll be along shortly.'

She grasped his hand tightly and smiled at him through moist eyes. The stretcher was elevated into the back of the ambulance. Lorraine kept her gaze on Jerry as their hands parted. One paramedic mounted the ambulance and sat next to Lorraine, picking up the piece of paper that lay on her stomach.

The doors closed and the ambulance slowly departed, picking its way through the police personnel and vehicles.

'Senor, where was the fatality you mentioned?' a police officer asked, breaking Jerry's gaze.

'It's over here,' Jerry replied. 'Near the dam.'

The police and another paramedic followed Jerry along the jungle path to the plastic shredder, and the remains of Adam.

'I'm afraid that there is not much left. I guess his body jammed the mechanism and stopped the motors. I've looked at the main breakers, and they have all burnt out.'

Robert was cold, wet and shivering. He had been drifting in and out of sleep for hours. Although the water level had dropped to his waist, he couldn't sit down and had to hang onto the cold, wedged, metal impeller shaft all night.

He became aware of some noise. Was it the generator or a vehicle engine? He wasn't sure, but there could be someone out there. What if it was the person who had pushed him in here? Christ, he didn't care. He needed to get out of here.

'Hello! Hello!' he shouted weakly. He stretched his arm under the water to try and find his discarded shoe, scrambling around, splashing and turning. He found it below the impeller, stood up and started banging the side of the tank.

'Hello! HELLO!' he shouted, louder this time. He banged again and again on the side of the tank, occasionally pausing to hear if there was any response.

He heard talking in the distance, and it seemed to be getting louder. Suddenly the door wheel began to turn. The access hatch opened and plastic pellets and water flooded out onto the feet of the grinning face of Jerry Hawkins. 'Of all the digesters in all the world you had to be trapped in mine!'

Chapter 16

Robert was staring at his computer screen. He had documented all the events of the last few weeks and was working on an outline for a new novel.

He was reading an email from GM Butler Oil & Gas.

'Dear Mr Howdon,

GM Butler Oil & Gas would like to apologise for the involvement of this company in certain unfortunate events that took place in Port Bata over May and June this year. We believe we have a comprehensive and generous action plan to address the concerns of the Mayor of Bata, the U.K. Government and the International Ocean Protection Agency. We have restructured our corporate divisions, and we also plan to introduce a more stringent regulatory regime to all our work.

We thank you most sincerely for assisting some of our staff in uncovering some of the events noted above. We wish to recognise your valuable contribution by offering you an award of £500,000.

This award is for you to use as your own, but we request that you demonstrate discretion over this period whilst work is underway to undo the wrongs that have been done. This includes any discussion with, or reports to, any news agencies, including television, press or any form of social media, that discloses any sensitive information or intellectual property belonging to, or is in any way designed to harm the reputation, or otherwise, of, GM Butler Oil & Gas.

Unfortunately, if we receive any evidence of a breach of this implied trust, GM Butler Oil & Gas would have no other option but to pursue legal action.

I sincerely hope we are not need to resort to such actions.

Yours sincerely,

Laura Coleman (GM Butler Oil & Gas Senior Legal Manager).'

It was countersigned by Jim Arnold, the CTO of GM Butler Oil & Gas.

Robert stared at the screen. 'What is this?' On the one hand, they were thanking him for uncovering the problems Hugh had caused under their watch, and on the other, they were making a legal request that amounted to a gagging order. Although half a million pounds would be a welcome sum and allow him to retire and concentrate on writing, he felt his freedom of speech was being compromised. Where would that leave him with his novel? Any details that could be associated with GM Butler Oil & Gas might see him facing litigious actions.

Did that put his friendship with Lorraine and Jerry in jeopardy? Could they still meet socially or would that raise suspicion of corporate lawyers?

Robert had left Port Bata two days after the incident at the production facility. He had several police interviews and was requested to attend any hearings should there be any prosecutions. He hadn't heard of any and news of the whole affair was strangely absent. Apart from tweets about his book, any communication about the incident was noticeable only for the paucity of information available!

Robert decided he would seek legal advice before accepting the "award", but at the same time, he felt that he probably would accept the offer.

#

The sky was clear and blue, although the summer mornings were starting to feel autumnal. Lorraine and Jerry took the opportunity to have a cosy lie-in. Lorraine's apartment had spectacular views over London, and Jerry gazed out at the view from the bed. Jerry was happy, probably for the first time in years. Contract work across the world had dragged him from place to place, leaving him no time to meet people and enjoy any meaningful relationships. His affinity to Lorraine was as much a surprise to Lorraine as it had been to him. Neither were particularly empathetic people, but they had both demonstrated their caring natures at a time of crisis. He felt content.

'Jerry, you are okay about this?' Lorraine asked, turning on her side to look at him.

'What, marrying you? Sure.'

'No, silly, getting married in my old Church in Westbury.'

'Yes, of course. Why did you ask?'

'Well, you seemed very nervous last week when we went to have my banns read. I thought you were maybe having second thoughts.'

'Now who's being silly?' Jerry rolled over, took Lorraine in his arms and nuzzled her neck.

'Hmm. Well, that's okay, then.' She whispered in his ear.

'Oh, Jerry I can't wait to meet up with everyone again. You know, it's been a month since we saw Robert.'

'Yes, well you can stop idolising him now you are with me,' he murmured, rolling back into his position next to her on the bed, sporting an obviously fake pout.

'Of course, I'm not idolising him, I only have eyes for you,' she giggled and turned to kiss Jerry on the lips. They held the moment until Lorraine turned back and leant over the bed to pick up her mobile phone.

'I've had a reply from Jane. She, Robert and Lucy, and Juan all are coming,' she said excitedly.

'That's good news.' Jerry smiled. 'It will be good to catch up with them.'

'Oh, and I've invited Bartho and his sister,' she added. 'I'm glad they got some compensation out of this awful affair.'

'Yes, and it's good that the fishermen's families got some compensation, and closure too,' Jerry agreed. 'I spoke with Juan last week, it seems he is doing well.'

'Ah, the lovely Juan,' she said, faking a moonstruck expression.

'Apparently, the clean-up work is being done by the team at Bata University,' Jerry continued, pretending to ignore her. 'They have all the technology there, and Juan had been given the responsibility to monitor the work and report on progress. He's been advising us, that is our company is taking his advice on board and progressing well. Good for him. He has been through a lot.'

'I think we all have, darling,' she replied. 'Who from our company is leading on this clean-up?'

162

'I've no idea although they could have outsourced this, but I no idea who they report to.'

'Ahh, possibly Jim directly then.'

'Juan said the remains of the gyre had been sprayed with detergents, and a huge floating inflatable pontoon has been put in place to contain all the plastics in a small area. Juan is monitoring the area for bacteria, and the plan is that the plastics will be lifted out and taken on board a ship.'

'And your idea of digesters on a ship will be used to digest the plastics. How ironic is that?'

'It's only a prototype, but I hope I'll get to see some royalties if it takes off,' Jerry laughed. 'I doubt it, but it's still the first use of one of the new digesters on a ship. Juan also said that all this had been a big news story in Bata. It was reported that a rogue employee – I guess he means Hugh, was doing things he shouldn't have been. He had been sacked and then died at his own hands, trying to cover his tracks.'

'Well that's not far from the truth,' Lorraine replied. 'Awful man.'

'But there has been no mention in the press about you creating the little monsters in the first place.'

Lorraine glared at him. 'That's not fair,' she said. 'I wonder what Jim will have to say about all of this tomorrow. It's the first monthly board meeting since the reorganisation, and our last before the big day.'

'Two firsts for me this month then,' laughed Jerry.

#

'Good morning ladies and gentlemen, and welcome to this GM Butler Oil & Gas board meeting,' Jim began. He was chairing the first board meeting since the merger and reorganisation of the new company. They were meeting in the GM Agro-Tech's conference facilities, now owned by GM Butler Oil & Gas.

'Before we get started, I'd like to introduce two new members of the board. To my right, we have Lorraine Bellamy, who is our new GM Research Director. And also Jerry Hawkins, our new Director of Overseas Operations.'

'Welcome Lorraine and Jerry,' Jim added, looking at Lorraine. 'I should also inform you that Jerry and Lorraine are getting married at the end of the month, so at next month's meeting, we will have a Mr and Mrs Hawkins attending. Today is a double celebration.'

The table erupted in applause and Jerry, and Lorraine nodded thanks around the table, slightly embarrassed.

'Please note this isn't a prerequisite for the board. You can be married to other people,' he smiled.

Lorraine looked around. Apart from the changes to the corporate logos and notice boards, the place was identical to the last time Lorraine visited. Jim had taken over Hugh's old office to use while he was at this site and had only just had it redecorated. The police had impounded Hugh's computer and sealed the room. However, some agreement had been reached, and the room was now accessible.

It had been a month since the incident in Bata, and she had been on leave, recovering from her injuries. She had started to get involved in work over the last week and had been discussing plans with Arthur, regarding her career in GM Butler Oil & Gas and spending the rest of her time planning her imminent wedding.

She heard Jim continue. 'Yes, welcome to you both, and congratulations. Jerry as well as acting as Head of Overseas Operations will also be responsible for scaling up from the Equatorial Guinea facility to other sites across the region.

'To date, media coverage of the digester has been very positive. There has been a lot of interest internationally, and sales from within the consortium are incredible.

'Laura, would you mind giving us an update on our current legal status? I don't think I have to remind everyone that this information is highly confidential,' Jim added, looking around the room.

'Sure, Jim. Thank you.' Laura stood up. 'There has been a great deal of activity around damage limitation to the consortium and GM Butler Oil & Gas,' she began. 'We have agreements with the Chief Executive of Plymouth University, The Chancellor of Bata University and the Port Bata Mayor's Office. Of course, the universities are embarrassed over the involvement of their professor of Marine Biology, and the Mayor is concerned about the possible loss of investment should confidence in the activities of petrochemical companies in the region come under scrutiny. Therefore, we have distanced ourselves from Mr Hugh Wilkinson's activities, and his link to the universities has not been acknowledged.

'With regards to the plastic gyre: the news of the fishermen's deaths and the student incident has largely been confined to Equatorial Guinea. We have provided compensation to all the fishermen's families, where known, under a non-disclosure arrangement.

'However, the students' parents were broadly uninterested in the event and ignorant of the actual danger on the gyres. It has generally been understood that their children hit flotsam in the sea and were splashed by some toxic algae bloom. All have recovered fully. None of the students has left the University course. If anything, the feedback we've received from them is that most had found it an important environmental lesson.

'However, we have started to assist the Bata University clean-up operation. We are doing this under the supervision of the port authorities and a representative of the UN's Ocean Governance Initiative. Again, this activity has been met with praise, both for our handling of the incident and for our ownership of and proactive response to the clean-up operation by our consortium colleagues.'

'Thank you, Laura.' Jim stood up. 'If I may, I'd like to add a little here.' Laura nodded and sat down.

'I want to thank Laura and the teams working towards getting these agreements and getting the clean-up started. We need to understand that we have been fortunate. Within UK waters we would have come under the jurisdiction of the UK Government, under both EU and UK laws regulating the release of genetically modified organisms. However, these issues at the gyre were outside the UK and EU, and we have not contravened any existing regulations.

'It's worth noting that although government consent is needed to release genetically modified organisms in the environment, these consents are only necessary for medical trials or GM food trials. However, there are no requirements for us to register genetically modified bacteria to use in containerised digestion and therefore nothing to control the release of the by-products into international waters.'

'If such rules were in place, I doubt that we would have survived this. Luckily for us here, but unfortunately for the world, there is no global governance of our oceans.

'I think we can agree that there needs to be a consortium of nations, probably reporting to the United Nations, which would manage the use and abuse of the world's oceans. We will work with UK government departments to assist where we can here.

'From the police report I have read; all of our staff have been vindicated. None are accused of being involved in the activities that Hugh undertook. Out of this terrible episode, there is some light, and we will be stronger because of this.

'I'll be leading the regulatory work, taking this on personally, although each of you and your teams will be involved with the process at some stage.' Jim paused.

'Arthur would you like to bring us up-to-date with your news, please?'

'Yes, of course, Jim,' replied Arthur. 'I'll be forming two GM divisions, Operational Support and GM Research, and will also support GM Regulation, which Jim will head. As you heard earlier my colleague, Lorraine, will lead the GM Research Division and report to me.' Lorraine nodded her acknowledgement.

'Operational Support will maintain support to our production colleagues, but within our Research Division, we will also be investing in developing bacteria that can digest many more types of plastic.

'The plan here is that we can combine these, as a cocktail if you like, to ensure maximal efficiency. Plastic digestion depends on the bacterial strain and the type of plastic being digested. Most of our attention to date has been on PET digestion, but there are many more plastics out there, such as Styrofoam, polystyrene, polypropylene, polyvinyl chloride etcetera, which we cannot currently completely digest with existing bacterial strains.

'We will work closely with Jerry on this matter, to ensure that optimal digester conditions can be maintained.'

Jim stood up again. 'Thank you, Arthur. I'm sure you won't mind me mentioning that, although Arthur wanted to retire, I have persuaded him to stay on a little longer, until summer next year so he can head up this immediate and important work. I am very grateful to Arthur for agreeing to this.' Jim smiled at Arthur and patted his shoulder.

'An exciting part of the work of the Regulatory Division will be to look at ways to actually turn off plastic digestion and to prevent other plastics being digested accidentally. We have received a government grant to assist in this research.

'We will also develop phages that target each of these strains individually, so that we have an antidote, if you like, in case any of these strains get out of hand. We also have an armoury of detergents and antimicrobials at our disposal to use in the future if necessary.

'We also plan to work with the plastics industry to find a way to degrade plastic only when we need to. For example, we don't want useful plastics to be accidentally digested while it's still in use. But when that item outlives its useful life and we DO want to digest plastic, how can we then turn digestion on, and any preventive mechanism off? Within the constraints of a digester, this isn't an issue, but we've just seen that this type of bacteria can survive outside digesters. We need a strategy to overcome any longer-term issues here.'

Jerry smiled wryly. It was his observations at the village about the digestion of the power sockets, which he had raised with Lorraine and Jim that had initiated the new research. Arthur was leading this work for now, but Lorraine was also heavily involved in the study, ready to step in when Arthur retired.

And it was Arthur who took the discussion forward. 'We think a modification of the plastics themselves will assist in the prevention of unwanted bacterial digestion. This may require a process whereby passing the "protected" plastic through a UV light, for example, that will neutralise some of the bonds in the plastic, allowing bacteria to digest them. But we need to work with the plastics industry on this.

'Work is currently at a very early stage, but as long as we contain the bacteria in the digesters, we shouldn't see any real issues.

'I have given the government and the Mayor my assurance that none of our strains will exist outside any of our production facilities.' Both Lorraine and Jerry looked at each other. Jerry frowned, and Lorraine quickly turned away.

Jim spoke again. 'There is an on-going issue that in our handling and dispatch of the bacteria IS-23, we, or rather Hugh, may have contravened EU regulations, but the government and EU would rather not prosecute due to the importance of the use of digesters to clean up plastics. We must keep to our part of the bargain and eliminate all GM Bacteria strains from the sea and clean up any residual microplastics.

'Of course, GM Butler Oil & Gas has also agreed to pick up GM Agro-Tech's liabilities here.' Jim paused and took a sip from a glass of water. 'Jerry, could you bring us up to date on your areas of responsibility, please?'

'Hello, everyone,' Jerry said, a little nervously. 'I'm new to board meetings, so excuse me if I seem a little nervous. I'm Jerry; responsible for ensuring the scaling up of more digesters at more sites, and the safe operation of these.' He paused. 'As you have heard, that might be more challenging than some people think.' He smiled nervously.

'However, the other very good news here, is that GM Butler Oil & Gas is in a leading position both in generating digesters, where we have produced the first working models and for cleaning up the environment.

'In fact, we are lobbying the UK government to increase the tax on plastics made from petroleum, so that recycled plastic becomes more attractive. Currently, new plastic is still cheaper than using recycled plastics. This isn't completely altruistic, as we'll be pushing the use of recycled plastic for our own commercial benefit, given that some of our by-products can be used to generate new plastic. This is a big part of our future planning.

'Within the next week, two more digesters will be deployed and installed at Bata, in some available facilities that have been locked up and have been storing plastic that has been imported from neighbouring countries. This also addresses our agreement with the Mayor's Office, helping them to clean up.

'I'm pleased to say that we can still be innovative. Just last week a retired Oil tanker was re-commissioned to assist the clean-up of the plastic gyres and rubbish patches at sea. However, to negate the need for the ship to bring the plastic to land, we have installed a digester on board, and it is being used to digest plastic right next to the gyres, without transporting them to land. The other technology that we've been looking at is miniaturising the digesters. We have got them down to the size of a small car. This would be particularly useful for plastic bottle banks, or areas that generate a lot of plastic waste. Maybe in time, we could generate even smaller ones for the home.'

#

After the meeting, everyone congregated outside the room, where they were provided with refreshments. Everyone seemed quite positive, upbeat even, perhaps relieved that GM Butler Oil & Gas had weathered the storm so well.

Arthur led Lorraine out to a corner for a private discussion. Jerry came to join them, but Lorraine gave him a stare that indicated 'stay away'.

'Lorraine I'm just so glad you are well and are back to full health' Arthur grasped both her hands and shook them. Although they had had telephone discussions, this was the first time Lorraine had met Arthur face to face since the incident.

'I'm glad to be back Arthur, there is so much to do.'

'Lorraine dear, I wanted to thank you personally for the email you sent from Port Bata. You know that honest disclosure was well timed and helped us to get actions moving to limit the damage from this mess.'

'Thank you, Arthur,' Lorraine said.

'But there is a particular issue that needs some careful attention.'

'What's that Arthur?'

'Well, your friendship with Robert Howdon.'

Lorraine looked concerned. *What's coming next?* she thought.

'The lawyers are rather sensitive about a close interaction between one of our employees and any such writer, fictional writings.'

'I can understand your concern Arthur, but Jim was just telling us how much we are doing. We are acting responsibly, and surely that should be communicated.'

'I agree my dear of course, but on our terms and not by a fiction writer. Of course, he could spin the information he holds whatever way he wants. But we shouldn't authenticate his stories by a link directly to the organisation.

'I've told the lawyers that they had my guarantee that none of our staff will have any contact with Mr Robert Howdon or his relatives or indeed anyone in close contact with him. I'm afraid that includes his daughter and her friends. Please don't disappoint me.'

'Oh. Okay, Arthur. I understand'

'Come on dear. Let's go and join the others. Your wedding is causing quite a buzz at the moment.'

Lorraine walked over to the group, and she instantly became the centre of attention. Everyone was asking her about the wedding plans. Lorraine told them all about the wedding, the reception and meal plan, the dress and honeymoon, and then the arrangements for working in the UK and Jerry being in Equatorial Guinea. Everyone was interested in her plans, and nodded approval and hugged her.

In a quiet moment, Jerry came over and spoke to Lorraine. 'Lorraine,' he whispered. 'Do you remember when you ran the samples at the production facility before we saw Hugh and The Prof?'

'Yes, of course, I do,' replied Lorraine. She guided Jerry into a corner of the room, away from the others.

'Well, what strain did you find from those samples you took at that village?'

'Didn't I tell you? They were all IS-23.'

'How is that possible?' Jerry asked. 'How can the strains that you produced in a lab exist in that village? How could they have got there?'

'Well, actually one of the technicians mentioned that IS-23 was used at the production site before your time I guess. Maybe it contaminated the river?'

'Even if that did happen, I wouldn't think that the water would still be contaminated.'

'Well, all those rivers are connected to each other. I guess that's how Juan thinks they got downstream.'

'Yes, that must be it,' Jerry replied.

'That is why GM Butler Oil & Gas are investing so much money to decontaminate the village and shift all the plastics up to the production facility,' Lorraine assured him. 'You should see the place. It looks so much nicer. The river is flowing down to the sea again. There is no blockage of plastics or red water. It's actually clear.'

Jerry said, 'It still concerns me a little.'

Chapter 17

Pedro Costalles, the quality control manager, looked through the process sheet and the quality checks needed at each stage of the conductor processing operations at the small factory at Bata.

The production and stretching of the raw copper cable, the addition of the plastic insulation, the assembly and product sustainability, were all areas of quality control under Pedro's watch.

He was proud of his work and the reputation of his company. His role was quite a prestigious one, with a lot of responsibility, and it was one that his family and friends respected.

After eight years of operation in a jungle region north of Port Bata, on a tributary of the Rio Mbini, the plant had become a successful enterprise, both economically, and prestigiously because of the highly-acclaimed training programmes its staff received, and the high-quality standards applied to its products.

It was due to this success that within the last two years, the company had expanded, to double its manufacturing capacity and increase sales ten-fold, to a broader customer base.

It had been a while since the initial investors in the new enterprise had received their return on investments with good bonuses, and now Cable Eléctrico Fabricante De Bata was generating substantial profits.

The company was now providing 70% of all the cabling products sold across Mid Africa and was gaining an increasing role in the expanding domestic market. Their products were being installed in new homes, hospitals, warehouses and, more recently, the airline industry, via its servicing hub at Port Bata International Airport.

Many commercial aircraft across the region had their mandatory checks and services regularly carried out here. For many African Airlines, which are denied operational flight licences within European airspace, and therefore access to high-quality services in Europe, a good quality-servicing hub within Africa had become essential in keeping the airliners, the passengers and profits, airborne. Even larger airlines such as South African Airways and Ethiopian Airlines, with access to European airspace and services, had chosen the servicing hub at Bata.

Recently, Cable Eléctrico Fabricante De Bata had installed a new labelling machine. This printed the details and specification of each of the cables, and now also included a logo. It looked like a teardrop, but was, in fact, the outline of Africa, with a spot on the middle of the west coast, where the facilities were located. It embodied the company's pride in being the centre of cable manufacturing in Africa, and its aspirations to supply all of Africa. Their customers recognised this logo as a mark of quality.

The main products of Cable Eléctrico Fabricante De Bata were reels of electrical cable, between fifty and three hundred metres in length, and varying copper thicknesses to carry different capacity of amperage. This made the cables suitable for use in a multitude of areas from building to aviation. Pedro was on his way to see one of his juniors, who he had tasked with locating some reels of cable that had not been despatched. Pedro expected they had been stolen, so although it may have been a wild goose chase for the junior, he'd at least had an opportunity to explore the facility and buildings.

'Pedro, sir,' the junior called him over. 'I have located where the reels are stored and found some earlier and some later batches, but these reels are missing.'

'Thank you, but that we knew.' Pedro frowned. 'That is why you were sent to locate them. But do not worry, they may have been stolen. We'll tell security to increase their surveillance, or we'll take the cost out of their salaries.' He smiled.

'But sir, what I mean is, I did find the labels.' The junior held his hand out and showed him two cardboard tags.

'Well done. But where did you find these?' Pedro enquired.

'Over here, sir.' He led Pedro behind the first stack of twenty coiled cable reels stacked in a five-metre-high pile. The shaded area behind was damp and smelt horrible, acrid and acidic.

'Look, sir.' He pointed down to a congealed nest of bare copper wire, intertwined with what appeared to be melted black cable sheathing. It was half the size of the original reel.

A red coating covered most of the cable, thicker in some areas than others, and it had also begun to encroach on some of the other stacks of reels.

'What the hell happened here?' exclaimed Pedro.

'It seems to be very damp,' said Junior. 'Maybe that's because of the recent heavy rain?'

'Yes, and maybe the overflow from the river,' agreed Pedro. 'But how does that explain the damage?'

They both walked up a slight incline towards the river, where water was drawn to flush dust and impurities from the final cable product. At the top, next to the river, Pedro stared in surprise.

The river was choked with plastic. It covered the river from one bank to the opposite shore. 'How did that happen?' Pedro muttered.

'Could it have been washed down, sir?' the junior suggested.

'Yes, yes maybe,' Pedro said slowly. His eye was drawn to the dark gaps between the plastic. He bent over to take a closer look and moved some plastic apart and alarmingly, the water looked red.

#

'Hello is that Robert?'

'Yes speaking,' Robert replied.

'It's Juan, how are you, sir?'

'Hello, Juan, it's good to speak with you. How are you keeping? Are you looking after my little girl?' he laughed.

'Si yes sir. We are both keeping well.'

'How is your work going Juan? Is the clear-up going well?'

'That's why I rang sir. It's going well with the clean-up at sea, and that it seems to be the focus of the company.'

'I sense a "but" coming Juan.'

'Si. The village of Ngaba has been cleaned up.'

'Ah, that's good Juan. Good work.'

'But sir after the heavy rain last week, I visited, and the river is full of plastic waste and red water again.'

'Really how so? There's no production further upstream that could contaminate the water?'

'Si I agree, that's what I thought. But after looking at the maps, there may be a contamination reservoir further upstream that we do not yet know about. But I fear that the issues we are seeing may be a bigger clean-up than first thought.'

'That sounds worrying Juan. But how can I help? Surely you need to speak with Lorraine or Jerry.'

'Si I tried, but I cannot get through.'

'Really let me try later and see if there is an issue. I only spoke with Lorraine last week, lots of changes at her company maybe they changed phones numbers or something.'

'I tried her mobile as well sir.'

'Okay, I'll try. I sense there is something else Juan.'

'Yes. Robert, I have received reports that a cable manufacturing company along a tributary of the Rio Mbini has contaminated cable reels.'

'Contaminated with this IS-23 E. coli strain?'

'Yes, possibly sir. I need to sample and analyse. But they report the contaminated red water.'

'Can't they be disinfected?'

'Possibly sir but apparently they have already been sold and installed.'

'Really? Where? What installations are they used at?'

'These have been installed into aeroplanes at the Port Bata service centre at the airport. And they are used all over the country. I'm afraid that this is getting bigger than I can assist with.'

'Hmm, I agree. But thank you, Juan. Let me make some calls. And I'll get back to you.'

'Okay, sir. Bye.'

'Bye Juan.'

#

'How was dad?' Jane enquired when Juan told her of the conversation.

'He was good, helpful and thoughtful as usual,' he smiled.

'You're worried, aren't you?' Jane said.

'Yes, I'm concerned that things are getting out of hand.'

'Darling you do worry.' She held his hand. They had been together since the incident, mainly supporting each other, but hadn't yet become a regular couple.

'Juan, how have you really been? I mean, since the incident?' Although Juan's features had returned to healthy, tanned and smooth skin and all the bloating and redness had subsided, he still bore some deeper scars.

'I'm good,' he said slowly. 'I think the work that I've been given is really good therapy. It's keeping me busy, and I think we are making a difference now.'

'But are you really okay?'

'Yes, I think I am, but honestly Jane, I saw some awful things in the water, and I was worried we wouldn't survive.' He paused. 'I really thought we'd die there at one point.' A tear welled in his eye.

'I know,' said Jane. 'I did as well. The only difference is that you were brave, and you got us all through it. You saved our lives.' Juan smiled shyly, and perfectly naturally Jane leant forward and kissed him slowly on the lips.

#

Lorraine who was sitting next to the telephone picked it up promptly when it rang. 'Hello.'

'Lorraine?'

'Yes. Hello Robert,' Lorraine cheerfully replied.

'Hello, Lorraine. How are things?'

'Oh, Robert things are going well here, how have you been?'

'I'm good. But I've just come off the phone with Juan. He couldn't contact you, and he is getting concerned that there is more work to do out there, he wants to make you aware of.'

'Ah Robert, thanks for ringing,' she paused. 'Things have got a little difficult recently.'

'How so?'

'Jerry and I have been talking about this matter. We were trying to think of a way to approach this with you.'

'Oh okay, go ahead Lorraine. What is it?'

'On Monday Jerry and I was told by Arthur not to have any contact with you and Juan. Apparently, the lawyers want us to keep a distance from you in case of any stories you may write or company information you might disclose. Of course, this makes communication and social calls difficult. We're bound to talk about some of our business and the contaminant.'

'Actually Lorraine, I can sympathise. I've had a similar request. I've been offered half a million to keep quiet.'

'Oh, Robert. That's great! Are you going to accept? I guess that if you did, we could still be in contact. We have the same confidentiality agreement then.'

'I'm still undecided. But I've had a conversation with Juan that concerns me about your company's activities.'

'How so?'

'He has told me that the Mbini River has tainted water again and water has contaminated a plastic plant that provides products to airport, planes and hospitals across Africa.'

'Oh my god, that's terrible. Perhaps if we get the decontamination team out there, we can clear this up.'

'I think it may be too late for that. This cable and other products have already been shipped and likely installed. Tracing them will be difficult. Of course, the equipment that's left should be decontaminated. But it seems the river keeps getting contaminated and the village Ngaba is blocked up again with plastic and red water. The source of this needs to be determined and dealt with.'

'Again really?' Lorraine exclaimed, sounding disappointed.

'Yes. But I think this issue has got bigger than your company. I don't think I can sit by and watch this get out of hand with a gagging order over me.' There was a pause.

'Robert,' it was Jerry's voice.

'Hello Jerry, I didn't know you were there.'

'Sorry I just got the other phone when Lorraine picked up. This is very difficult. We respect your decision, of course, Robert, but Lorraine is correct in that we can't speak with you or have any association with you.

'Also, we can't use this information you're giving us because our lawyers will know we have spoken to you or Juan. I'm sorry we can't do anything to help. Take care, Robert.' Jerry then hung up.

Robert was stunned.

Robert looked into his writing desk drawer, and took out the contract sent from GM Butler Oil & Gas. He folded it in two and tore it into very small shreds.

Chapter 18

'Lucy, I don't think I have any choice in the matter,' explained Robert. 'What's your opinion?' Robert finished after recalling the conversation with Lorraine and Jerry.

'Well, I'm shocked that they dropped you like that, after all you've been through. But it's hardly their decision, they are, after all, just following the company line.'

'I do agree with your decision.' Lucy had listened intently to Robert's news around the contract and Lorraine and Jerry's stance. 'You're caught between a rock and a hard place. If you signed the contract, we'd be richer, and maybe still have some social connection with Lorraine and Jerry, but you would lose your professional integrity. If you write anything about what you know or any of your experiences you've been through, the company could potentially see this as an infringement of the terms of the contract.'

'What's strange is that Lorraine and Jerry were told to keep their distance regardless of whether I signed the contract or not. Seems like their company wants me isolated from them regardless.'

'Whatever you choose I'll support you, you know that.' Robert smiled, leant over and kissed her.

'Thanks. That's why I love you so much.'

'I think I need to go back out there to talk with Juan, help him find out where the source of the contamination is.'

'Shouldn't the company do this?' asked Lucy.

'I don't think they will. Juan is not getting any response from questions he is asking. It's like their focus is on the sea clean-up, nothing else.'

'If you are going, I have some things you can drop off to Jane.'

'Can't you make it as well darling?'

'I'm sorry, I won't be able to at such short notice.'

'No problem. I'll only be gone a couple days,' Robert replied.

#

Aleta avidly watched the Africa News broadcast at both midday and at seven each evening. She always updated Bartho, her brother, on the latest developments, often accompanied by her own opinions. It was from her avid interest in the news that her eye had been drawn to the incident involving Jane and Juan, which brought her to meet Robert Howdon.

Through this direct interaction with Robert and Lorraine, Bartho and Aleta had been invited to London to attend Lorraine and Jerry's wedding next week. Aleta thought these English were "pan bendito" and kind. They had been at the award ceremony at Malabo, where Bartho had received a medal for trying to save his crew and where he also received compensation, a sum that would more than assist them in his enforced retirement.

Aleta was looking forward to the trip. She had bought her wedding outfit weeks in advance, had told all her friends, and anyone who would listen, about the wedding in England, which was also going to be attended by her friend, the well-known author Senor Robert Howdon. Aleta, however, remained nervous about her first flight, but she knew she had no option but to conquer her fear if she wanted to attend the wedding in England.

'Bartho, there has been another terrorist attack on domestic flights,' she called to him while sitting in front of her TV, a few days before their trip.

'Don't worry Aleta, it's still safer than driving,' he replied.

Africa News had covered stories throughout the week of suspected terrorist attacks on flights over Africa. Several organisations were blamed, from Boko Haram to the Muslim Brotherhood, but no one had yet claimed responsibility. In total, two hundred and ninety-seven lives had been lost. Curiously, the number of flights cancelled or grounded due to technical failures had also risen, but this hadn't been reported on with the same enthusiasm as the terrorist attacks. Crash investigators were working on the wreckage, but lack of access to some remote crash sites meant that no definitive cause had yet been ascertained.

Aleta's nervousness wasn't eased any by such news or Bartho's dismissive comments. She continued watching the broadcast, fumbling with her rosary beads with increasing nervousness as the flight day loomed.

#

Robert greeted Juan warmly when he arrived at the Escuelas Nauticas Bata campus. Jane came running over from the notice board where she was standing with some other students.

'Daddy, hello!' She hugged him and spun around him.

'Whoa!' Robert laughed. 'I've missed you too honey.'

'So good to see you, daddy. How long are you going to be around?'

'I'm afraid I'm here for two days and then I have to get back for another book signing. I'm starting to enjoy them now,' he laughed.

'Your dad and I will see if we can find the source of the contamination. We only have the rest of today and tomorrow, so we should get started.'

'I agree. Jane do you want to come with us?'

'I'd love to dad, but I have a diving class in an hour. Hopefully, see you later though.'

'Okay, darling. Right, Juan let's go.' Robert kissed Jane goodbye, and he and Juan left towards his hired car.

'Right Juan where shall we start?'

'Sir, I thought we could start at the cable processing site.'

'Good plan, can you direct me?'

'Sure,' Juan replied. 'I have also brought my map. I have plotted the production facility and the cable plant on here. Thought we might be able to follow the river back up.'

'Good thinking Juan.'

'Thank you, sir.'

'Hey, Juan I know you now, please call me Robert.'

Juan directed Robert to the cable production facility low on the river Mbini.

'Robert you know this facility is on a tributary of the river just a mile from where they join at the harbour.'

'Really I hadn't seen any river empty into the harbour.'

'The last half mile or so are through pipes under the roads.'

'Ah that explains it,' replied Robert.

They pulled into a car park without any security and walked up to a prominent building.

At the reception, Juan asked for a Senor Pedro Costalles, the man who had raised the concern with the police, who in turn had asked the university to investigate.

Within a minute, a short, smart man walked into the reception area. 'Hola senor Dougan de la Universidad,' he said and held out his hands to greet Juan.

'Sí, y este es el Señor Robert Howdon, él es inglés,' Juan replied.

'Ah hello Senor Robert,' Pedro said shaking Robert's hand.

'Good to meet you, Pedro.'

'Please, where is the water source in question?' Juan asked.

Pedro led them up an incline to a bank of the river Mbini. The river was tainted red and had clumps of plastic across to the other bank and more plastic clusters further along the river. Juan took some samples in his bijoux glass sample bottles.

'Sir how long has the river been like this?' Juan asked.

'I only noticed it a month ago, but I suspect much longer. I don't tend to come up here,' he answered.

'Where are the contaminated cables you reported?' asked Robert.

'Si this way.' Pedro directed then back down the incline towards the storage area as Juan put the samples in his bag.

Soon they were at the cable storage area. It was evident what reels were somehow melting, and others had also started to be affected.

'It looks like all these reels have been exposed to the contaminant. These will have to be destroyed. None should be used,' suggested Robert.

'Si,' Pedro replied. 'This area has been quarantined. Nothing is being issued from this area.'

'When was the last reel issued from here?' asked Juan.

'Over a month ago when I first found the melting one there,' Pedro pointed to the partially destroyed cable.

Juan took samples here and asked, 'Sir where do you now store your cables?'

'Ah, we keep them within the warehouse now.' He added, 'Have you any idea what is causing this?'

'I'm sorry sir we cannot say for sure where it originates from. But your idea of storing inside is good.'

The two men thanked Pedro, washed their hands and headed back to the car to drive up the mountain towards the production facility.

#

Robert and Juan drove in up to the security barrier at the production facility. They were refused entry initially, but a security supervisor walked over. As he approached the car, he recognised Robert from the last visit.

'Hello Senor,' he said bending to look at them both through the windows. 'I'm afraid without a pass you cannot come in but what is the purpose of your visit?'

Juan spoke up in Spanish and explained that he worked for the University of Bata and was under contract to clean up some areas and he needed to sample the river at the facility's dam.

The security guard went to the phone and rang someone. He came back smiling and let them through. 'Please just take your samples and leave. You have been allowed twenty minutes.'

'Thank you, gracias,' Robert and Juan said.

'I thought we might have been turned away,' Juan said.

'Yes same,' said Robert, 'but we had to try, thankfully we managed it.'

In the gantry office, Jerry put the direct security telephone down and turned to the table to continue the review of the blueprints with designers around the table.

The river at the top of the dam was still completely coved by plastic as Robert last remembered. They cleared a patch of plastic away and took a sample of the water. It looked clear.

'We'll analyse this, but it looks good Robert.'

They walked around the dam to the water source and to water flowing from the dam as far as they could get. They saw no evidence of contaminated water. Juan took several more samples, and they both headed back to the car. Robert had a morbid curiosity of the state of the shredder on the dam weir. As they headed towards the weir steps, he could see that a new river inlet had been installed with a safety cage over the machinery next to the path.

They left the facility and headed down the mountain towards the harbour. 'Wait,' said Robert. 'Let me see the map.' He pulled over to the side of the road and took the map from Juan.

Robert traced this location on the map of the river Mbini and traced the river down to the cable facility. They were indeed on the same river, albeit on a separate tributary. He then went back to the top of the river on the map and looked for roads en route to the production facility that was also on the river.

'Yes, this is it!' Robert exclaimed. He gave the map back to Juan and pulled back onto the road continuing down the mountain.

'What is it?' asked Juan.

'There was another disused production facility that Lorraine had stock delivered to, but when we visited it, it was closed, and we never went in. It's on the river, and it's worth a look.'

Robert took a sharp left turn and drove along a single bumpy track. Within minutes they had arrived at the abandoned facility. The gates were securely locked. Robert followed the line of the fence to where it turned back towards the jungle. Deeper into the jungle Robert spotted a tree that had fallen, crumpling the fence. It looked easily traversable.

'Look' Said Robert. Walking towards the tree. Juan followed

They climbed over and pushed their way through ferns and small bushes towards an asphalt area. The asphalt was crumbling and long grass broke through the surface. A pre-fabricated, single storey, concrete building, was now visible at the end of an asphalt drive. 'I don't believe it's been used for at least a year,' Juan suggested. With the heat and humidity, the jungle had reclaimed the facility and gave the appearance that it had been abandoned for much longer.

'I agree.'

As they approached the buildings, they heard running water and headed towards the sound.

The light became brighter as they entered a clearing in the jungle. Robert and Juan were met with a shocking site. A substantial square concrete pool had been built to retain water from the water running downstream. The water flowing in was evidently clear; however, the water flowing over the weir, barely visible due to the mounds of plastic being retained in the concrete pool… was tainted red.

'This is it!' exclaimed Robert. 'This is the source of the contamination.'

'Magnifico!' exclaimed Juan. 'This explains both the contamination at the cable production plant and the village of Ngaba. Good work Robert.' Juan smiled. 'We need to get this decontaminated before it spreads down other waterways.'

'Yes. I'll contact the university, and they can talk to GM Butler Oil & Gas Company.'

'Yes, that sounds like a good plan, especially as I'm not supposed to contact them directly.'

As they headed back to the car, they passed the corporate signpost, Robert glanced at it, and then again. 'Now look at that.' Robert said as he stopped looking at the stained sign informing visitors.

The corporate sign, as expected stated, 'River Mbini South. Production facility of Butler Oil & Gas. Site Manager Jim Arnold.'

'Jim Arnold,' Robert said. 'What was he doing here and using the strain?'

Juan had rung ahead and told Jane that they would meet her at the campus for a late lunch and then get the samples analysed. Once he had finished the call, he asked, 'Oh actually Robert do you mind if we take the long route back and go past the harbour please?'

They were almost at the bottom of the mountain, and the harbour was en-route to the campus.

'Sure. What are we looking for?' Robert asked as they headed to the harbour.

'I want to see where the river discharges into the sea,' replied Juan

As they approached the harbour, they could see a red tint to the shallow water. The sea along the harbour appeared a darker shade of red. Robert pulled the car over.

They got out and looked over the harbour wall. A hundred yards from where they were standing two pipes discharged water directly from the Mbini River. The water was again stained red.

'Robert do you see anything alarming here?'

'Apart from the red water? No what am I missing?'

'Well sir, there are well-known reports of animal and plant species being carried thousands of miles in ballast water.'

'What do you mean?'

'At harbours big container ships have to pump water in as the load is lifted off to keep the ship at the same level against the harbour, keeping it level and buoyant.'

'If a ship travels empty or partially empty, it will carry water from one port to another. When containers are loaded onto the ship, all the water is pumped out as cargo is added. Any water-borne species from one port becomes introduced to another. You know that large container ships, such as these, can carry as much as three million litres. It has been well documented that Zebra mussels were accidentally introduced to the Mediterranean from the Baltic, it now displaces native aquatic life and blocks water intake pipes.'

'Juan, are you suggesting that any IS-23 E. coli in the water here could be pumped into the ships here and discharged at ports around the world?' Robert asked.

'Yes, sir.'

From where they were sitting, they could see two container ships further along the harbour wall surrounded by the same tainted water.

Robert took his mobile phone out of his pocket and launched the web site for the Port Bata ship passage itinerary. 'His eyebrows raised as he read the information displayed. Turning to Juan he solemnly declared; 'One of those ships is due to travel to Las Palma Gran Canaria this week via six other African ports. The other is travelling directly to Port Santos in Brazil.'

#

The big day had arrived, and Aleta and Bartho arrived at Bata International Airport and checked into their flight to London at the Ethiopian Airlines check-in desk. They were taking a short internal flight to Malabo and then flying on to London Heathrow.

They were a little late to the departure lounge as Aleta was carrying crochet needles and scissors. As Aleta had never flown before, she was quite perturbed at her belongings being confiscated at security, but the result was that they now had to rush to board the plane.

'If only you had packed them in the big case,' Bartho had murmured as they rushed along through the departure lounge corridor and joined the queue on the Passenger Boarding Bridge. Eventually, they were shown their seats by a friendly stewardess, who assured Aleta that she would be fine and that she would make it her mission to ensure Aleta was looked after.

Forty Minutes into the flight to Malabo, the sunset was streaming through the port windows of the DC10 and everything was calm. Bartho and Aleta were enjoying a glass of red wine. Aleta was finally starting to relax.

Suddenly the plane appeared to hit some turbulence. The lights flickered as the aeroplane fell and lifted several metres. Aleta screamed and held on grimly to her crucifix. She spoke under her breath in Spanish and crossed herself. Others in the cabin smiled, and some chuckled, raising their eyebrows at the novice's reactions to a little turbulence.

The other passengers continued to chatter and eat and drink. The glasses occasionally shook, but the passengers accepted the minor irritation. No one seemed particularly perturbed, apart from Aleta.

But the plane again dropped and lurched from side to side. The seat belt signs pinged on and cabin crew rushed to their own seats, folding them down, and sitting, nervously facing the passengers. Aleta tightly held Bartho's hand. The plane jolted sharply again, and the oxygen masks fell to head height and swung erratically. Aleta screamed, and all the passengers now became nervous.

The plane levelled and steadied again.

#

For several weeks the plane's electrical cable had been stored in hot, humid conditions. It was stamped with a batch number and manufacturing code, and a logo that was a teardrop icon of Africa. The contaminated water that had washed the cable of impurities had now been active for a month. Microscopic bacteria, thriving in a hot, humid atmosphere, installed in the fuselage, had been slowly dissolving the plastic that insulated the copper cable. The cable was now live with electrical impulses, connecting the flight controls to the

187

actuators, the pumps and motors around the aircraft as it flew on its way to Malabo.

Tonight, directly below the passengers feet, the digestion of the plastic sheathing had reached a critical point. Copper wire was now bare. Electrical ions raced from the bare positive cable across to the earth disrupting the communication of the flight controls.

The electrical sparks increased in frequency and the heat intensified and started to burn the bundles of Eléctrico Fabricante cable. The Africa quality stamp bubbled and melted into drips that fell onto other burning plastic sheathing below. A thick, pungent smoke slowly rose from the burning plastic, through the hull void into the cabin foot- well. As the flight controls begun to fail, the passengers slowly became aware of the danger below their feet.

THE END

References

Equatorial Guinea
Genetic Modification
Plastics Generation
Plastics Pollution
Plastic Eating Bacteria
Container Ship Ballast
(n.d.). Retrieved from
https://www.fleetmon.com/ports/bata_gqbsg_8169/#tab-
companies-in-port

Brent, J. (2012, Nov). Springer. Retrieved from
https://link.springer.com/article/10.2165%2F00003495-
200161070-00006

British Plastics Federation. (2018). Retrieved from
http://www.bpf.co.uk/Sustainability/PET_Plastic_Bottles_Facts
_Not_Myths.aspx

Davis, U. (2016). Plastics and chemicals they absorb pose
double threat to marine life. Phys Org. Retrieved from
https://phys.org/news/2013-01-plastics-chemicals-absorb-pose-
threat.html

Electrical Installation WiKi. (n.d.). Retrieved from
http://www.electrical-
installation.org/enwiki/How_an_electrical_cable_is_made

Fiona Harvey. (2018, Feb). Environment. Retrieved from The
Guardian:
https://www.theguardian.com/environment/2018/feb/05/whale-

and-shark-species-at-increasing-risk-from-microplastic-pollution-study

Julie Masura1, J. B. (2015, July). Laboratory Methods for the Analysis of Microplastics in the Marine Environment: Recommendations for quantifying synthetic particles in waters and sediments. Retrieved from https://marinedebris.noaa.gov/sites/default/files/publications-files/noaa_microplastics_methods_manual.pdf

Lorch, M. (2016, March). Scientists Just Discovered Plastic-Eating Bacteria That Can Break Down PET. Retrieved from https://www.sciencealert.com/new-plastic-munching-bacteria-could-fuel-a-recycling-revolution

National Ocean Service. (2018). National Ocean Service. Retrieved from https://oceanservice.noaa.gov/facts/microplastics.html
Takada, D. H. (2013, may). Ocean Health Index. Retrieved from Microplastics and the Threat to Our Seafood: http://www.oceanhealthindex.org/news/Microplastics

The Guardian. (2016, Aug). Retrieved from fish-confusing-plastic-debris-in-ocean-for-food-study-finds: https://www.theguardian.com/environment/2017/aug/16/fish-confusing-plastic-debris-in-ocean-for-food-study-finds

The Great Pacific Trash Vortex. (n.d.). Retrieved from https://wharferj.wordpress.com/2013/01/21/the-great-pacific-trash-vortex/
The Ocean Cleanup. (2018). Retrieved from https://www.theoceancleanup.com/

UK Gov. (2013). Retrieved from Genetically-modified-organisms-applications-and-consents: https://www.gov.uk/government/collections/genetically-modified-organisms-applications-and-consents